A
Second
Slice of
Magic

A novel
by A.G. Mayes

Cover image by Lisa Seng
www.studiointhegarden.com

This book was printed in the United States of America.
Copyright © 2017 A.G. Mayes. All rights reserved.

ISBN-13: 978-1981816033
ISBN-10: 1981816038

www.agmayes.com

To my husband.
To my family.
To my dogs.
To everyone who loves pie
and believes in magic.

Acknowledgements

A special thank you to Char Torkelson for editing and formatting my manuscript. Thank you for being an incredible leader for the Monday night writing group. I feel lucky to be a part of it. Thank you Marilyn, Anne, Fay, Patty, and Ruth for all of your support and encouragement.

Thank you to my wonderfully talented cousin Lisa Seng for designing the book cover.

Prologue

There was a cottage nestled in the snowy countryside at the bottom of a hill. From the outside it looked like it belonged in the pages of a storybook, but inside life was no happily ever after.

Dennis and Stan, a father and son, were playing chess by the fire. A woman with greying brown hair and sharp green eyes walked in. The younger man felt all the muscles in his body tense.

"Did you get it?" she asked.

"No," Stan answered quietly. Dennis stared at the board.

"What?" she asked sharply. Both men flinched. "We would be in control of all the magic in Hocus Hills by now if you two blundering buffoons didn't fail at every little task." She spoke as though all the magical residents in the town of Hocus Hills were just objects for her to possess.

"Alice set us back when she got caught. I should have never let her convince me she could control people through altered magic spices. She didn't have the skills, and I don't think her heart was in the mission. She was too distracted by the loss of her sister." Sometimes Brenda just liked to hear the sound of her own voice.

"We can try something else," Dennis offered, never taking his eyes off the chess board.

"Of course, we'll try something else," Brenda snapped. "We still have two days before Ivan gets here. We'd better have some new recruits by then. That shouldn't be hard. There's always magical people who want more than to hide out in a small town."

She paced up and down the room. Her shoes clicked sharply against the floor. Stan watched his mother pace.

"Erma — she's going to be the problem," Brenda was muttering under her breath now. "But think of how happy Ivan would be if we got her magic."

She went to the fireplace and threw in a couple of logs. Sparks flew, and heat poured out as the flames rose higher.

Chapter 1

I wiped a bead of sweat off my forehead with the back of my hand and surveyed the display case. It was packed full of pies. Only ten minutes until we opened.

Aunt Erma came out from the kitchen carrying a blueberry pie, her specialty. She wore a hat with felt antlers and jingle bells.

"What do you think? Do we have enough?" She stood next to me.

"Not if business keeps up the way it has," I said. We'd sold out every day this week. Now that Aunt Erma was back and could teach me her secret recipes with her magic spices, customers had been pouring through the door.

I went back into the kitchen to bring a load of garbage out to the dumpster. I jumped back a little when I saw a black and white spotted cat sitting just outside the back door in the alley. Just one month ago, before I knew anything about magic, Aunt Erma had been the cat in the alley. An evil woman named Alice had turned her into a cat and tried to steal the spells for Aunt Erma's magic spices. Now, Alice was in some kind of magical jail. The exact details about what magic jail meant were still a little fuzzy to me and no one seemed eager to fill me in.

"Meow once if you're human," I said in a low voice. She meowed, and my eyes widened.

"Are you talking to a cat," Henry appeared from around the corner. Henry was my almost boyfriend. We had been dating for a few weeks, and I think we were nearing that point in the relationship when I could begin to use the B word.

"How do you know that this isn't a person?" I asked, greeting him with a quick kiss.

"I'm magic," he said with a smile. "And I know that's Mrs. Peterson's cat."

I leaned in for a kiss but pulled back when I saw Violet rushing towards us. Violet and I had a rocky relationship. Back when I was running the pie shop alone, she kept coming in looking for Aunt Erma and making accusation. At the time, I thought she was a health inspector. Violet's eyes were wild and her usually perfectly slicked down tight bun was a frizzy mess.

"Where's Erma?" she asked.

"She's inside," I said. "Is everything OK?"

Without a word, Violet rushed through the backdoor into the kitchen. I looked at Henry, and he shrugged. We followed her inside.

"What's wrong, Violet?" Aunt Erma had rushed over and put her hands on Violet's shoulders.

"It's happened," Violet said.

"Take a breath and tell me everything." Aunt Erma's voice remained calm, but I could see fear in her eyes.

"Dennis and Brenda. Stan. The missing spice bottle. They've finally figured out how to make the altered spices on a larger scale, and they're testing them out," Violet's words rushed out. Dennis and Brenda were Stan's parents. Stan had been the delivery man in town until a month ago when we found out he and his parents were working with Alice to try to steal Aunt Erma's magic spices.

"Oh no." Aunt Erma's arms dropped to her sides, and she took a step back to lean against the kitchen island. "What can I do?"

"We need you to help us track them down," she said. "We've been working on it since they disappeared, but they've

4

evaded us so far. You might be able to trace the magic better since it was your magic in the first place."

"Let's go to Flora's and figure out a plan," Aunt Erma said, leading us out to the front of the shop. The pie shop was supposed to open in two minutes, and already there were a few early birds waiting outside the front door. They perked up as they saw us approaching.

"Sorry, folks. We're going to be opening a little late today." We all stepped outside amid the groans. "Come back later for your pie and a free cup of coffee," she said, locking the door behind us. I could still hear a few grumbles as the people shuffled off down the street. If only they knew the reason.

Aunt Erma had let it slip once just how dangerous it was that Stan had the bottle of spices. We had gone to Sal's bar one night to celebrate. We were celebrating a lot of things these days — our reunion, the fact that Aunt Erma wasn't a cat anymore, years of missed holidays and birthdays. Aunt Erma had introduced me to a drink called a Fairy's Foot. I was a little hesitant because the name did not sound appealing at all, but it was actually quite delicious. Like drinking a chocolate milkshake. The smooth sweet flavor hid the fact that the drink packed quite a punch, and by our second glass, Aunt Erma had completely lost her filter and was sharing information about her love life that would have made me blush if I wasn't already flushed from the drink.

"Make sure you find someone with good hands," she was saying firmly. "The hands are just as important as the…"

"No," I clapped my hands over my ears. "Tell me something else."

She giggled. "Fine." She took a deep breath. "I'm worried."

"About what?"

5

"The missing spice bottle. Spice number three. Three, three, bo, bee," she paused to take a sip of her drink. "The things they can do with that magic." She shook her head.

"Like what?" I asked. My experience with the spices was limited, but I didn't understand what would be so bad about them.

"The magic in them is so powerful because of the secret ingredient. That's why you have to be careful to use just a little bit in the pies and make sure you're focusing on the proper intention when you add them. I'll explain it more to you one day. Maybe when I'm sober-er." She clinked my glass with hers and began talking about highly inappropriate things again before I could ask her what the secret ingredient was.

Once we were inside Flora's, she led us back to a small door in the back of the shop. I hadn't noticed this door before. That wasn't surprising. Flora's shop was packed full of books. It had probably been behind a stack or a shelf the other times I had been in there.

We went down a dark narrow staircase to a room below. It was warm and cozy with a floor-to-ceiling bookshelf filled with old volumes. Mr. Barnes and Lena were already there. How had they beat us there? There was a quiet anxiousness in the room.

Henry and I sat in chairs next to Lena, and Violet strode quickly to the front of the room. There was a computer with a large screen on the desk. I smiled at Lena, and she flashed a quick smile back at me. Violet stuck a thumb drive in the computer, and a black and white video started playing. It was a group of people walking along in a line down the street. They took slow even steps, and something about the sight made me shiver a little. Henry reached over and took my hand. Then suddenly everyone stopped walking. People looked around as though confused, and then the crowd dispersed.

"They must be having trouble making the effects last very long," Mr. Barnes said. The video skipped ahead, and Stan's parents popped up on the screen. Even in the grainy footage, I could recognize them. They were walking along, stopped, and looked straight into the camera.

"That's strange," Flora said. "They know the camera is there. Why don't they hide themselves better? They could have erased the footage if they really wanted to."

"I thought so too," Violet said. "The only conclusion I could come to is they wanted us to find them. That can only mean one thing. They're trying to draw you out, Erma."

All of our heads turned towards Aunt Erma. Her eyebrows were pinched together with worry, but she quickly rearranged her features into a brave face.

"If they want me, they'll get me," she said with a determined edge to her voice.

Chapter 2

"I'm going with her," I'd said amongst the protests.

"Neither of you is going anywhere until we figure out if this is a trap or not," Flora pulled out her stern librarian voice that made me shrink back a little.

"I have to go," Aunt Erma said almost matching Flora's firm tone. "Someone has to stop them before they figure out how to make the effects last longer. I'm best suited to do that since it's my magic they're altering. You know how dangerous it could be if they're successful. For everyone. We need to stop them before it spreads."

Everyone was silent for a minute.

"I think she's right," Violet said.

"Susie, I'm not sure you should go, though," Lena said. "I think I should go along with you."

I bristled a little at her slightly condescending tone. I might be new to this magic thing, but I knew I could be helpful. I had taken karate for three years when I was in elementary school. There were some problems magic couldn't solve.

"We should all go," Mr. Barnes chimed in.

"That might draw too much attention," Violet said.

"Susie will come with me," Aunt Erma said firmly. "She's ready, and I know you'll all be here ready to back us up if need be." Everyone nodded. "But that won't be necessary," she added with a confident smile towards me. I noticed that when Aunt Erma talked, people tended to agree with her.

"And I'll keep an eye on you through the security cameras," Violet said, pointing at the computer screen. She had paused the image on Stan's parents, and I glared at them trying to build up my confidence. If I could keep myself from being afraid of their image, then I could definitely take them on in person, I assured myself repeatedly.

I winced as I realized Henry was gripping my hand tightly. "Hey," I said, gently. I put my other hand on top of his and began to carefully pry his fingers loose.

"Sorry," he said, softening his grip. "I hate the thought of you going, but I understand why you are. Just promise you'll be careful, and call me if you need anything."

"Of course." I kissed his hand, and he smiled at me in a way that made my heart flutter.

The crowd dispersed, and Henry squeezed me tightly before heading off to his job at the nursing home.

"Come with me." Aunt Erma grabbed my hand and led me to her car.

"Are we going now?" I asked, unable to keep the panic out of my voice.

"No," she said. "There's something I want to show you." I got in the car.

"Hold on, I'll be right back." Aunt Erma ran to the pie shop. She only seemed to have one speed, fast. A minute later she reappeared with her dog Mitzy close at her heels. Mitzy was a brown ball of fluff with expressive eyes and boundless energy. Her large brown eyes showed that she understood when you talked to her. Sometimes I found that a little unsettling.

Aunt Erma opened the back door and Mitzy hopped in. Her tail was wagging so hard I thought she might take flight.

"Mitzy loves a good car ride," Aunt Erma explained. She heard her name and somehow took it as an invitation to leap from the back seat and into my lap.

"Hi Mitzy," I said flatly. I loved Mitzy, really, but I was still getting used to this furry licking creature who lived life like she did a shot of espresso every hour.

Aunt Erma drove through Hocus Hills. The town looked like Father Christmas had thrown up on every street corner. Lights twinkled on every tree and bush and along the front of every shop. I didn't see a single door without a wreath and a very elaborate winter wonderland had been set up in the town square complete with nine reindeer, several elves, and Christmas fairies. There were banners all over town advertising the snowman building contest happening next weekend. "Erma's Pies" was one of the sponsors, and Aunt Erma had been making me practice my snowman building skills for the last two weeks.

"The middle is not round enough," she'd said about one of my practice snowmen that I'd built in the park next to the ice rink.

"But it's getting kind of cold out here," I'd said. "Can I try again tomorrow?"

"One more time," she said. "The competition is fierce, and we need to make a good showing of it."

"But I can't even win since we're sponsoring." I could hear a little whine in my voice, and I was ever so slightly embarrassed, but being this cold made me revert to my young self.

"I know we can't win, but we have to build one in support of the competition, and we can't embarrass ourselves either," she said taking apart my snowman. It turns out that when it comes to snowman building competitions, Aunt Erma is like the worst overbearing pageant mom out there.

"Can't we just use magic?" I asked as I carefully rounded out the middle ball.

"Magic is forbidden at these competitions," she said. "At least until after the judging when everyone makes their snowmen dance," she giggled. "Lena made hers twerk last year. I didn't even know what twerking was until then."

10

"Yeah, Lena's pretty hip." I rubbed my hands together through the mittens before reassembling my snowman.

Aunt Erma took a step back and sized it up. "Not bad," she said with a curt nod. "Tomorrow we'll work on making the perfect facial expression."

"Great, can't wait," I said a little flatly.

We drove out of town and hit the highway.

"Where are we going?" I asked. The car was finally warm, and I sank back into the brown velvet seats of Aunt Erma's old light blue car. Mitzy had settled down in my lap. Her previous excitement seemed to be wearing off.

"You'll see," Aunt Erma said. She turned up the volume on the radio and Christmas songs filled the car. She sang "Rudolph the Red Nosed Reindeer" at the top of her lungs. I'd learned how to sing from her — off key, but enthusiastic. Her enthusiasm was infectious and soon I was singing too. Mitzy groaned disapprovingly and moved to the back seat of the car. I would have to remember this trick whenever Mitzy was annoying. Sing loud, and she'll leave. Who would have known?

We exited the highway and turned down a narrow, wooded road. Then we turned down a narrower dirt road and finally Aunt Erma pulled over as far as she could, which wasn't far on this skinny stretch, and put the car in park.

"Is this it?" I asked, looking around expecting to see something more than trees and snow.

"Yes. Follow me." She got out of the car, and Mitzy flew over the seat to follow her. I got out and wrapped my red coat tighter around my body. I shivered against the cold air.

"Are you going to tell me what we're doing yet?" I hurried to keep up with her. She was half a foot shorter than I was and twice my age, but she walked so fast! I'd asked her how she walked so fast before. Was it magic, I had asked her.

"Not magic," she winked at me. "Yoga."

11

I really had to start going to more of Mr. Barnes's yoga classes this winter. Or I was going to have to stop walking with Aunt Erma.

Mitzy was frolicking in the snow and still managed to keep up with Aunt Erma. I hopped over sticks and tried to step exactly in Aunt Erma's footprints, so the deep snow didn't go over the edge of my short boots. We didn't seem to be following any path, and I couldn't imagine a house would pop up in this deserted woods. Aunt Erma stopped so abruptly and I was hurrying so fast behind her that I bumped into her, unable to stop my momentum.

"Sorry," I said, scratching my nose which had bumped against her tall fuzzy white hat.

"We're here," she said with a satisfied nod.

"We're in the middle of the woods," I said, glancing around wondering which of us was going nutty.

"There," she pointed ahead of us.

I squinted and saw a small tree that had green and red and silver balls hanging from the branches. Even in the dead of winter, it still had all its leaves. The winding branches danced in the breeze and the baubles tinkled together.

"What is it?" I asked, hoping she wouldn't just answer with the obvious "tree."

"It's a magic tree," she said, providing an ever so slightly better explanation than I was hoping for.

"I don't understand," I said. "Why does it have ornaments on it?"

"I decorated it for Christmas," she said with a sheepish shrug of her shoulders. I nodded. That was a very Aunt Erma thing to do. Then I wanted for more information. She carefully touched one of the leaves, and the branches began to rustle a little harder. That was strange, the wind hadn't picked up.

"You've probably heard a few murmurings around town about how powerful my spices are," she began slowly.

"I've heard a thing or two," I answered.

"I've always been pretty powerful," she said. She wasn't bragging, just stating a fact. "However, I found a way to be more powerful." She gestured to the tree with a flourish of her arm. "It came to me in a dream one night. After I saw it, I woke up, got in my car, and somehow, I just knew where to go. I ended up here. This tree contains more magic than I ever even knew existed. You can feel it."

She grabbed my hand and put it on the trunk of the tree. I felt the tingling of power course through my body.

"How does it work?" I asked. I held my hand there even after she took hers away. I was enjoying the feeling of power.

"For some of the spices, I scrape off a little of the bark, and for others, I use the leaves," she said. "It's tricky with this much power to get the intention just right. That's why I keep it simple. Some of my spices spread love. Some happiness. Some make people more helpful. I never do anything big or complicated because the more complicated the magic, the more likely it is that something will go wrong. And when magic goes wrong it can get really ugly." She shuddered a little.

"What do you mean?" I asked. I wanted specifics. I was tired of all of this, "Things can go bad with magic" stuff. I needed answers now.

"Ok, I'll tell you a story." She thought for a minute. "A while back when an elf was running a factory. Well he was part elf, like we're part fairy," she added. "If he was full elf he would look like an elf, pointy ears, the whole bit, but there are many of us who are part something, and we can just blend in with people who are one hundred percent human."

I nodded. I began to worry that this was going to be a long-winded story, and it was cold outside. I looked around for

Mitzy. She was still frolicking around the trees. Maybe it was because she was enjoying it. Maybe she was just trying to stay warm.

"His factory made clothing," Aunt Erma continued. "And soon greed got the best of him. He used magic to produce more and more clothing. He made his workers move faster and faster until they were collapsing in the factory. Then to make matters worse, the clothes started acting up."

"The clothes acted up?" I asked, incredulously.

"Yes, sweaters were opening and closing closet doors, socks were banging against the side of dressers. It was a disaster. People everywhere were panicking. There was a huge rush on exorcisms." Aunt Erma shook her head. "The magical enforcement team was busy for months un-enchanting all of the affected clothing and altering people's memories, so they thought it was all a strange dream."

"Good story. Can we go back to the car now?" I was jumping up and down trying to keep my blood from freezing in my veins. I looked down. My feet were still there, but I could no longer feel them.

"Yes, yes, let's go back to the car," she said scooting back through the trees. Mitzy eagerly followed us.

"Why did you take me here?" I asked, a little breathless as I struggled to keep up again.

"I wanted you to know where this was. In case anything happens to me," she said, matter-of-factly.

I stopped in my tracks. She was about a hundred yards ahead of me before she realized I wasn't following anymore. She turned back. I started walking again, and she waited for me.

"Is this really that dangerous?" I asked, trying to keep the quiver out of my voice.

"We'll be fine," she said firmly. "Plus, we have a vicious guard dog on our side." Mitzy yipped in agreement. I tried to smile, but I couldn't shake the anxious feeling hanging over me.

Chapter 3

My head was spinning during the drive back to the pie shop. My thoughts began to blur as the car warmed up. Mitzy settled in my lap. The snow melted off her fur and was soaking through my pants. My eyes snapped open. "They aren't going to turn you into a cat again, are they?" I asked.

"No, they wouldn't do that again," Aunt Erma reassured me as she merged onto the highway.

"Does the Morning Pie Crew know about the magic tree?"

She shook her head. "You're the only one I've told. It's safer. The fewer people who know, the better."

"But I thought you guys shared everything." I couldn't help but feel a little proud to be in on the secret, but it scared me a little too.

"Everyone has secrets," she said. She pressed her lips together and kept her eyes fixed to the road.

I stopped prying. I stared at the road too until we got back to the shop. The crowd had gathered outside again, and people began to stir when they saw Aunt Erma's car pull up to the curb out front.

"Come in, everyone," she said as she shuffled between them to unlock the front door.

"Someone was looking for you." Nadine, one of our regulars, whose blonde curly hair was always gathered in a poof on top of her head said to me. As far as I could tell, her job in town was to spread gossip.

"Oh yeah? Who?" I asked following her through the door.

"I don't know. Some guy."

"Henry?" I asked even though I figured he would call me if he were looking for me.

"No, some curly haired guy I haven't seen before." She shrugged.

"I guess this mystery man will have to come back if he wants to talk to me." I went back to the kitchen and stopped in my tracks.

"Mom," I said.

"You recognize me. I'm so touched," she said, barely looking up as she sliced a peppermint cream pie. My mom's brown hair was just a shade lighter than mine. Unlike mine, it was smooth and perfectly styled on her head. Instead of her usual business suit, she wore jeans and a dark green sweater.

My mother had gone back to the city a couple weeks after Aunt Erma had become human again after being a cat. We had a wonderful week where our days were full of baking and gossiping. We were a regular holiday special. Then the bickering began, and the comments under our breath, and my mother decided she had to get back to her clients at home. I didn't blame her. It was a lot of intense family time after a long absence.

"She'll be back soon," Aunt Erma had reassured me as I had watched her car drive away with a lump in my throat. I had been enjoying the gossiping and reminiscing. It had been so long since I'd seen my mother laugh that much.

That was less than two weeks ago, and here she was again. I guess I didn't have anything to worry about.

"Erma called and asked me to come help at the pie shop while you guys went on some sort of mission." My mother began cutting the next pie more forcefully than was actually necessary.

"We have to go…," I began.

"No," my mother cut me off still keeping her eyes on the pie. "I don't want to know. I know it has to be dangerous. I could tell from Erma's tone. It's best if I just worry here instead of knowing the specifics. I'll just serve pie and worry."

Ah, my mother the martyr.

"How long are you here for?" I asked.

"I booked a room at the inn for three nights, but we'll see," she answered. My mother preferred to stay at the local inn instead of squishing into Aunt Erma's apartment with us.

Aunt Erma had already fulfilled the orders of the crowd out front. The angry grumbles had turned into happy chattering as people drank their free cups of coffee and talked about their holiday plans.

"I'm taking my cats to see Santa," someone said.

"My sister is coming to visit with her four children, and they're all staying in my one bedroom apartment," I heard someone else say.

"My husband is in a Christmas play, and he wants me to go watch all twelve performances," another voice chimed in.

I heard a familiar voice say my name. I saw him in the crowd, but it didn't register because he was a familiar face in an unfamiliar place. I was shocked and speechless for a moment.

"Josh," I finally managed to croak reaching out to hug him.

"Hey, Susie," he was warm and smelled like sawdust. He held me for a second longer after I had let go.

"What are you doing here?" I asked, taking a step back to look at him. His dark curly hair had gotten a little long. He had dark circles under his brown eyes, and his usually rosy cheeks were pale. "Is everything OK?"

"Hal has me working at a big remodel in Mavisville," he said. Mavisville was just the next town over. "It should take a couple of weeks."

"That's great. We'll definitely have to get together a few times," I said.

18

"I need to talk to you," he said.

At least four people in the store stopped their conversations to openly stare at us.

"Let's go outside." I grabbed the sleeve of his coat and led him towards the front door.

"Who is that?" I heard someone whisper loudly as I opened the door.

"Beats me. I'd bet an old boyfriend," someone else said.

I glared over my shoulder in the general direction of the voices. Josh and I had been coworkers back home. We had grown to be good friends, but it was never anything more than that. Josh was the one I'd call when I was having trouble with a relationship, and I would give him insights on the people he dated whether he asked for it or not. I hadn't really talked to him since I'd left — just a couple quick text messages that didn't really say much.

I wrapped my grey sweater more tightly around myself and faced him. I thought longingly of my red coat hanging on the hook at the back of the kitchen. Why had I suggested going outside? The mid-December wind was biting against my skin. Oh yeah, outside was the only place we had a shot of not being eavesdropped on. However, if anyone could lipread, we were in trouble. All of the customers in the shop were blatantly staring through the window. They might as well have their noses pressed against the glass.

I took a couple of steps back toward the flower shop next door so we were at least a little out of sight. I'm not sure there was anywhere completely out of sight in this town though.

Josh stared at the ground for a minute.

"Is everything ok?" I asked again. I wanted this to hurry up, so I could get back to the toasty warm kitchen.

"So, you live here now?" he asked looking up and down the street.

"I think so," I said with a shrug. "I haven't really figured it out long term yet. I live here for now, I guess."

"I'm glad you got to reunite with your aunt," he said. Josh had heard my sob story more than once about my long-lost Aunt Erma. Usually it was after a bad day at work or a fight with my mom and a few beers.

"Yeah, it's been nice," I said. It was silent for a minute, and I was about to tell him I had to go back inside.

"You didn't even say goodbye to me," he said suddenly meeting my eyes for the first time since we'd gone outside.

"What?"

"We were friends. Maybe more. At least I thought we were," he said the last part more to himself than to me.

I opened my mouth. Nothing but air came out.

"Was I just imagining it? I kind of thought we were on track to get together. I thought you felt it too. Hell, I've loved you since I saw you fix that hole on the side of the Morrow's house. You were fearless at the top of the ladder while the rest of us were too chicken to climb that high."

I remembered that job. I had been terrified too, but I was new at Hal's Handyman Services, and I wanted to show off in front of my new coworkers. Afterwards I'd had to excuse myself to the side of the house where I promptly threw up in the trash can. I thought back to my time with Josh. Had I missed the signs? Sure, we had been good friends. I would even consider him to be one of my best friends. I hadn't meant to drop him when I came to Hocus Hills, but finding my long-lost aunt, discovering magic is real, and trying to squash an evil plot to take over the world all takes up a lot of one's free time.

"Josh, I…" I paused for a minute. "I'm sorry I didn't say goodbye." It sounded lame when I said it. He looked at me expectantly. "And I'm sorry I haven't kept in touch better. It's been so crazy around here."

I didn't even know where to begin with his other confessions. There had been a time a few years ago when I thought about him that way. I'd even tried to flirt with him and hang out with him more than usual, but shortly after I began to have those feelings, he began dating a woman his sister set him up with. It was serious for a while, and I moved on too. I hadn't really thought about it since then.

I jumped when I felt a hand on my shoulder. I turned, and it was Lena.

"I hate to interrupt, but we have to get going," she said with a polite nod towards Josh.

"We?" I asked.

"I'm Lena," she stuck her hand out towards Josh.

"Nice to meet you, Lena. I'm Josh." He shook her hand. "I'm a friend of Susie's from back home."

She looked at me with raised eyebrows.

"So, we need to get going, huh?" I said.

"Right, yes," she said.

"Bye Josh. I'll call you later." I followed Lena inside trying to ignore the guilty feeling in the pit of my stomach when I looked over my shoulder and saw him watching me go.

The chatter inside the pie shop stopped immediately when I came through the door. No doubt they were all talking about me. I ignored them and went back to the kitchen.

"I'm coming too," Lena burst into the kitchen carrying her large yellow purse.

"Now, Lena," Aunt Erma began in a tone I knew meant she was about to try and talk her out of it.

"Don't you start with me, Erma. There's room in the car for one more. I'll drive." So that's how I ended up in the backseat of Lena's car clinging to the handle by the window with one hand and gripping the blue velvet seat with the other. Speed limits were merely a suggestion in Lena's world. I swear as we

21

rounded the corners, the car tipped up on two wheels. When I said this out loud, Lena told me to stop being so dramatic.

"You'll thank me when we get there and get this taken care of quickly," she said, speeding up as the light in front of us changed from green to yellow.

"Here, eat this," Aunt Erma passed a small square to me, and Lena popped one into her own mouth. I inspected the square before eating it. It was white with little green flecks in it.

"What is it?" I asked.

"It will protect you," Aunt Erma answered.

"From what, a car accident?" I asked.

"The magic."

I took a tentative bite. It tasted like salt water taffy, so I put the rest in my mouth and chewed. I always expected to hear wind chimes when I ate something magical, but to this date that had not happened.

In between muttering wishes for a safe arrival, I thought about what Josh had said. Henry and I were having such a wonderful time, but Josh and I went way back. He was comfortable in a way that only someone you've known a long time can be. He was like a thick warm comforter. But then with Henry there was a spark. People always said the spark doesn't last forever — that you need more in your relationship besides electricity. But the spark sure felt good right now. Maybe it would develop into the comfortable relationship I had with Josh. Maybe it would be even better. Plus, Henry knew about magic. There was a whole part of my new life that I wasn't sure if I could share with Josh. The people of Hocus Hills are very private about their magic, and I certainly don't blame them. You never know who you can trust, and if word got out that there were magic people in the world, there would be chaos.

We squealed into a parking spot on the street at the edge of town. I still wasn't any closer to figuring out my love life, and it didn't seem like the time to ask Lena and Aunt Erma for advice.

"We should walk in so we can sneak up on what's happening. Get a feel for what we're getting into," Aunt Erma suggested.

"Everyone take note of where we parked in case we get separated," Lena pointed to the street signs on the corner. My stomach flipped. In case we get separated? That thought hadn't even crossed my mind.

The streets were deserted. It was Saturday. Most towns would have people coming and going from the shops. We peeked into the window of a bakery. A bakery on a Saturday should have people buying their bread and donuts, but it was empty.

We kept going down the street. We walked close together, and I resisted the urge to reach out and grab Aunt Erma's hand for protection.

Everywhere was deserted. It was spooky. It was like every horror movie I'd ever seen, but even more surreal because it was real life. I kept looking around expecting a tumble weed to roll down the street.

"Where is everyone?" I whispered as we neared the center of town. The layout was similar to Hocus Hills except their town square was a little smaller, and there was a duck pond near the gazebo.

Lena shrugged.

"I don't know, but it can't be good," Aunt Erma said.

I stopped in my tracks. "I hear something," I said. They both stopped, and I held my breath as we listened. There was a sound coming from the church.

"We need more yarn," we heard a deep voice yell. The church was a large white wooden building with steps leading up to a set of dark wood double doors. We crept up the steps, and Lena pushed the door open a crack. She peaked inside.

"I think we found everyone," she said pushing the door the rest of the way open.

The church was jam packed with people of all ages. It was a flurry of activity, but I couldn't figure out what they were doing. Some people were rushing around the room picking up balls of yarn and moving them from one pew to another. Several people were knitting. Knitting? I noticed a large red circle in the middle that they were all working around.

"What are they making?" Lena wondered aloud.

"A mitten," a man with an armload of knitting needles yelled as he rushed past us.

"The world's largest," one of the women who was knitting called.

"Why are they doing that?" I asked. I almost felt dizzy from the frenzy around us. This seemed like more than just a quirky small-town activity.

"It must be part of the spell," Aunt Erma said.

"But why?" I asked. It seemed like such a strange activity, and not at all in line with their ultimate goal.

"It's probably an accident," Aunt Erma said. "They're too power hungry to focus on getting the spell right. They're frenzied as they alter the spices. It's very hard to get the intention right — takes a lot of finesse. They were probably trying to hit a kitten or flit off to Britain and somehow it came out to knit a mitten. That's why you should always keep it simple." She was speaking to me now. I nodded as I looked around at the chaos. I certainly didn't ever want this to happen.

"How are we going to break the spell?" Lena asked, jumping out of the way of a frenzied boy who was chasing the armload of yarn balls he had just dropped as they rolled across the floor.

24

"Do we need to break it?" I asked, looking around. I mean, what they were doing was crazy, but it didn't seem to be harmful. Unless they started capturing people inside the giant mitten once they finished knitting it.

"It could be dangerous to leave them like this. They won't be able to stop until they've finished no matter how tired they are, and some of them could actually work themselves to death," Aunt Erma said. OK, that sounded bad. She was surveying the scene intently.

"I'm going to need a kitchen to get the job done," she said. "Unless," she turned to Lena, "Do you have anything?"

"I told you you'd need me," she said as she fished around in her yellow purse. She set it on the floor, and her whole head disappeared as she leaned into it. I was tempted to grab her feet, so she wouldn't fall. I didn't know what exactly was inside there. I had asked her once how the magic purse worked.

"Oh no, dear, I couldn't tell you that. Your aunt may be ready to divulge all of her secrets, but I like to keep one or two up my sleeve," she had said.

"Ah yes, here it is," her muffled voice emerged from the purse a second before she did. She triumphantly held up an Erma's Pie box.

"You keep a pie in there?" I asked.

"You never know when you'll need one," she said. "Impromptu dinner party, afternoon snack, to stop crazed knitters."

Aunt Erma took the box from Lena and opened the lid. She took a deep breath.
"The triple berry. Yes, this one should work. The unaltered spices will counteract the altered spices they used," she said. "They're not all going to eat willingly. We're going to have to coax them."

Lena did some more digging in her purse and emerged with three plates, three forks, and a knife. We divided the pie. I watched Aunt Erma approach a young man who was knitting and offer him a bite of pie. He shook his head vehemently, his sandy brown hair flopping across his face. Without missing a beat, Aunt Erma shoved a bite into his mouth. His eyes widened so much I thought they might pop out of his head. He chewed and swallowed all the while making, "Mmmm," noises. Then his face changed. His brow furrowed, and he looked around.

"What's going on?" he asked.

"Don't worry about it," Lena said. "You're just having a strange dream. Go home."

The man shrugged and shuffled off.

"Alright everyone, understand the plan?" Aunt Erma asked.

Lena and I nodded. Then we all set off shoving small bites of pie into people's mouths. Most people I encountered were easily convinced to take a bite. They were probably hungry after all this knitting. The church began to clear out as people wandered back home.

"Aren't they all going to talk and figure out they had the same strange dream?" I asked Lena as I airplaned a bite into a young girl's mouth. Lena did the same with the girl's mother. The girl dropped the yarn ball she had been winding up and followed her mother out the door.

"Most of them will have forgotten about this completely by tomorrow. Only a few will have a distant memory of this strange dream," she said. "It won't be enough for them to put it together that it actually did happen."

"Some of them might be a little sore tomorrow from all the work," Aunt Erma said as she ran passed, chasing a man with gray hair and thick glasses. The man threw a ball of yarn at Aunt

Erma, and she tackled him and shoved the bite of pie into his mouth before he could stop her.

It wasn't easy, and I was bit at least six times, but we finally we cleared the church of all frantic knitters. I leaned against the wall and began planning which pajamas I was going to wear, the footy pajamas with the turtle print, and what I was going to eat, pizza with three sides of pie.

"We have to get all this out of here," Aunt Erma motioned to the giant knitted circle that was apparently on its way to becoming the largest mitten in the world.

"Why?" I asked. I didn't want anything to keep me from that pizza any longer than necessary.

"It's a lot harder to convince people it was a dream when they can come to the church and find two tons of yarn and a knitted circle as large as a parachute.

After we'd cleared everything, dispersing some of it and shoving the rest of it into the back of Lena's car, we headed back to Hocus Hills.

"What are those?" As we pulled into Hocus Hills, I pointed at a light pole plastered with sheets of paper.

"I'm not sure." Lena slowed the car down. Aunt Erma finished reading first and gasped.

In big bold letters, the signs said, "Tired of hiding? It's time to work for the Improvement of Magical People. If you're ready to step out of the shadows, stay tuned for more information from the IMPs." The flyers were plastered all over town.

"It was all a circus. They just wanted to get you out of town, so you couldn't stop them from doing this," Lena practically yelled.

Aunt Erma let her head fall to the back of the seat. "I don't know why we didn't see that before," she sighed.

A crew led by Violet was already pulling posters down.

"We were so focused on what you guys were doing, that we didn't even see this happen until it was too late," she said. "They worked fast. It was done in a matter of seconds."

Aunt Erma's brow furrowed. "Their magic is getting stronger."

"I know. The regular spells aren't working to clean it up, so we're doing it the non-magic way," Violet said.

I grabbed a bag and went to work pulling signs off the light poles and the sides of some buildings.

"Hey," Holly appeared by my side. "I heard you had some hunky curly haired stranger show up today."

"Hunky?" I asked.

"My mother's words, not mine," she said.

"How did she see him?"

"Nadine texted her a picture," she said as though the answer was obvious.

"What?!"

"I forgot you're still new to this small town living where everyone knows your business," she said. "So, what's the story?"

"Josh is a friend from back home," I said evasively. I quickly asked her about the latest book she was writing, and she was off telling me how she wasn't sure if she should kill off one of her favorite characters or not. I was off the hook for now, but at the end of the clean-up, we made plans for a girls' night out on Friday, and I knew there would be more questions then.

Later that night I was wrapped in my very large new red knitted blanket watching television when Henry stopped by. I struggled to get out of the cocoon I had wrapped myself in.

"Did everything go OK?" he asked after greeting me with a long hug.

"I didn't realize magic was such hard work, but yes, it went fine," I said. I was too tired to give him the details, and I was pretty sure he would have heard them already from someone in town. News spreads fast. Especially the news that you wanted to keep quiet. Just yesterday I heard Mrs. Lansbury yell across the street asking Mr. Kelley about his colonoscopy.

"Anything interesting happen before you saved the world?" his tone was strange, like he was trying to stay super casual, but his voice was too high and too tight.

"Oh yeah," I said, also trying to keep my tone casual as though I was just remembering something that I'd actually been thinking about all day. "A friend of mine from back home stopped by."

"Really?" he tried to sound surprised, but his acting wasn't that good.

"Yeah, we were coworkers. He came to say hi." I shrugged in what I hoped was a casual gesture.

"That's an awful long way to come to say hi," he said.

"He's working on a job in Mavisville for a couple of weeks," I said.

Just then Aunt Erma bustled in. "Oh, I'm sorry to interrupt. Henry, how are you?"

Aunt Erma's arrival saved me from an awkward conversation. Her glance out of the corner of her eye told me she knew exactly what she was doing.

Henry left after a little more small talk. He said he had some work to finish. I was the only person in town, other than his editor, who knew that he wrote the "Ask Elodie" advice column in the newspaper. I had asked him once if all the letters were sent in from people in town. He said some of them were, but some days there weren't any letters, so he would make up letters and then answer them as Elodie. "So, you set up a problem you know you can answer?" I had teased him. Then I began to quiz him about which ones he had written. "I'm not going to ruin the magic for you by giving away all the secrets," he'd said.

I felt bad for not telling him more about Josh, but I wanted to be able to process it more myself first. I hadn't figured out how to present the facts because I hadn't figured out how I felt about the whole thing.

The truth would come out eventually though.

Chapter 4

"Do you want another magic lesson?" Aunt Erma asked.

"Yes, please," I said. I hopped up off the sofa and sent Holly a quick message. "Gotta run. Got some pie learning to do." She and I had been texting each other while we watched the same reality show. "Tell me how it ends," I couldn't help but add.

With everything going on, I felt like the more magic I knew, the better. We'd been trying to sneak in as many magic lessons as possible, but it was hard to work them in when we were so busy with holiday orders.

Now that my mother was here, time for magic lessons would be even more scarce. Aunt Erma told me that my mother used to practice magic regularly, but I never saw that side of her. Even after we reconnected with Aunt Erma, she was still reluctant to embrace magic again. I think she blamed magic for failing her when she tried to use it to save my dad when he was sick. She wanted Aunt Erma, who had always been the most powerful one in the family, to help my dad, but she refused. She said the magic she would have to use was too dangerous. My mother cut her out of our lives after my dad died, and neither of us saw Aunt Erma for over twenty years. Now we were trying to piece our family back together.

Aunt Erma and I were both in our pajamas. She wore a rainbow striped fleece onesie, and I had on red flannel pants and a white t-shirt that said, "If I'm not smiling, bring me coffee." We put aprons on over our pajamas, and Aunt Erma pulled a ball of pie crust dough out of the fridge. She had assured me many times that there was a huge difference between the taste of a well chilled pie crust and a room temperature pie crust. A few times when Aunt Erma wasn't watching, I'd made pies without chilling

31

all the ingredients for the crust thoroughly. I couldn't tell the difference, but she always noticed.

"Let's make a banana cream tonight. Doesn't that sound good?" she asked, handing me the pie crust. I agreed and got to work rolling the crust out while she gathered the rest of the ingredients. I never ceased to be amazed by how many recipes she had memorized. I was lucky if I could remember two ingredients before I had to check a written recipe. Aunt Erma assured me that I would get the hang of it eventually.

She retrieved her box of magic spices from its hiding place behind a secret trap door in the back of the pantry. She had put even more protection spells on them to keep them safe from the IMPs.

The wooden box was painted purple and covered in a glittery glaze. There were twelve glass bottles inside. Each one was labeled with a number written in green. Bottle number three looked a little different from the rest. That was the spice Alice had stolen, and the original bottle was still missing. Aunt Erma replaced the bottle and created a new batch.

She pulled out a few of the bottles and quizzed me.

"What does this one do?"

I got most of them right. Laughter, encouragement, helpfulness, relaxation, love.

She was holding up Spice #8 now. I wrinkled my nose as I tried to remember what that one did.

"Honesty," she said when it became apparent I didn't have an answer.

"Right," I said, slapping my hand against the kitchen island. "That one can get you into trouble."

"Yes, you have to use it very carefully and in very small amounts. It's good for people who need to stand up to someone or get in touch with their feelings," she said.

I nodded as I put the pie crust in the oven to bake.

"Tonight, I think we should try mixing two spices together. That really takes some artistry," she wiggled her eyebrows at me. "Which two should we try?"

I picked laughter and encouragement. I felt like we could use both of those things right now.

We used instant pudding mix to make the filling of the banana cream tonight. Aunt Erma usually turned her nose up at such a shortcut, but she made an exception because it was late, and we were hungry.

"Here, put one dash of each spice in the filling," Aunt Erma said, handing me the two bottles. "Remember, your intention as you add the spice is just as important as the spice you use." There was a knock at the back door and Aunt Erma went to answer it. We had talked about the importance of intention before, so I focused all my energy on laughter and encouragement as I sprinkled the spices into the filling.

"I heard rumors there might be some pie to try in here?" I heard Holly's voice.

"Almost ready," I called.

"I considered your text to be an invitation," she said. She walked into the kitchen and surveyed the work we'd done. "I'll make the whipped cream," she offered, washing her hands.

"Who ended up together?" I asked. I was dying to hear what happened next in the reality show we were watching.

"Ben kissed Cici even though Matt is clearly in love with her, and Eddie asked Julie out on a date, but the show ended before she answered."

"No!" I said. "I can't wait a whole week to find out!"

Aunt Erma watched this exchange with raised eyebrows.

"Trust me, it's an addicting show," Holly told her. "You should watch next week."

"I'm probably going to be busy," Aunt Erma said.

As we let the pie chill in the fridge, Holly told us about some of her early magic memories. "My mother always taught me growing magic because she likes to grow fresh herbs and vegetables. Our garden always grew so many vegetables, and she would send me to school with bagged lunches packed full of green things. I would con my friends out of pieces of candy, and then I would use the growing magic to make the pieces of candy ever so slightly bigger." She gave a satisfied nod. "I was quite the rebel."

"I didn't know you were such a wild child," I laughed.

We didn't let the pie chill in the fridge for long before we cut large slices for each of us.

Aunt Erma took the first bite and let out a giggle. "I think you may have put a bit too much of the laughter spice in here," she said.

"I think you did a great job," Holly said after her first bite, "Really top notch. No one can spice a pie like you can. We should crown you pie spicing queen of the universe."

"Did I put in too much of the encouragement one too?" I asked.

"Yes," Aunt Erma snorted. "But we can try again tomorrow."

"I'll be back for that," Holly said.

I wanted to join the fun, so I took a bite of pie. The pie was quite tasty. We alternated between gushing over each other's fabulous qualities and laughing hysterically.

There was still room for improvement in my magical education, but the learning process was fun.

Chapter 5

Dear Elodie,

My sister recently moved back to town. She had lived out of state for the last fifteen years. I'm so excited about her return and want to invite her along to everything I do. My problem is the only thing she wants to do is square dance. She turns down all of my invitations and will only call me once a week to ask me to go square dancing with her. I'll be honest, I hate square dancing, but I'll go to be with my sister. I've tried telling her I would like her to come along to some of the things I invite her to, but she just dismisses me, saying she's busy. Am I wrong to be upset by this? Can I quit square dancing without quitting my sister?

Sincerely,
Round Peg in a Square Dancing Hole

Dear Round Peg in a Square Dancing Hole,

It sounds like you've given your sister every opportunity to do something other than square dance with you, and you've made your feelings known. It's possible she feels overwhelmed. If she's been away from family for fifteen years, it could take some adjusting before she's used to your invitations. Maybe she's getting just as many invitations from other family members. Also, if you keep doing exactly what she wants, she has no reason to accept your invitations. Maybe you can square dance with her one week and the next week you can tell her you're busy on square dancing night, but if she'd like to go to dinner with you a different night, that would be wonderful.

Ask and I'll Answer,
Elodie

The next morning, I woke up to the smell of pancakes. I took a deep breath and stretched out on the sofa. Mitzy, so excited to see movement, catapulted onto my face.
I yelped thinking for the umpteenth time that I needed to get my own place. I had been looking. Sort of. But part of me wasn't sure it was worth the effort. Was this just a temporary move or a more permanent one? The pie shop was fun, but I wasn't sure it was the place I was meant to be. I still required a fair amount of supervision, and I wasn't sure I would ever be able to whip out pies as fast and effortlessly as Aunt Erma.

"Oh good, you're up," Aunt Erma said peeking her head around the corner from the kitchen.

"Yup, thanks to the fuzzy alarm clock here," I pointed to Mitzy who danced around on the floor next to me. She was like that friend that everyone had. The one that thought you were better friends than you were. She never sensed my hesitation to reciprocate her affections.

"I made chocolate chip pancakes," she said, holding up a steaming plate.

"Yum." I was off the sofa now. I poured myself a cup of coffee. "What's on the agenda for today? Please tell me we're not tackling a town who's set on making the world's largest pot holder, are we? I'm still recovering from yesterday."

"No, nothing like that," Aunt Erma said. "At least not that I know of," she added.

"Look at this," I pulled up the side of my shirt to show her two small bruises on my ribs. "Someone jabbed me with their knitting needles. I guess I should consider myself lucky that they didn't skewer me."

Aunt Erma inspected the bruises closely, her brow furrowed. She ran her finger over them, and I flinched.

"That's not good," she said. "They shouldn't be able to hurt you."

"What do you mean? Was I supposed to have some sort of magical shield around me? Because I definitely forgot to wear my knitting needle armor yesterday. Do you think they make such a thing? Like giant thimbles for your body."

"They shouldn't have been able to hurt you because none of the magic from my spices should make people do that," she said. "Even in their altered state, plus you had the taffy."

"But aren't some people inclined to hurt other people? Maybe it was the person, not the magic," I said.

"Yeah, maybe," Aunt Erma said, but I could tell she was still concerned.

"Have you heard anything more from Violet?" I asked.

She shook her head. "And today we're not going to think about it."

"We're not?" I asked, my mouth full of chocolate chip pancakes. I knew if my mother was here, she would remind me that she raised me better than to talk with my mouth full, but the pancakes were just so darn good. They were light and fluffy, and the chocolate chips were melted just right. Aunt Erma had even topped them with whipped cream and shaped them like animals like she used to do when I was a kid. I was eating the ear off a dog when I noticed Mitzy giving me a disapproving glare.

"How does she know I'm eating the dog pancake," I wondered under my breath.

"Magic," Aunt Erma said with a wink. "Now today, instead of focusing on the evil plot to take over our beloved town, we are going to decorate for Christmas."

"Decorate? Even more than we already have?" I asked. I thought about all the tinsel we'd hung and the cardboard Santa cutouts in every corner of the shop downstairs.

"Yes, we're just getting started," she said sitting down across from me with her own stack of pancakes and cup of coffee. "We haven't even begun to cut out the paper snowflakes yet. Last year I cut out three hundred tiny snowflakes and hung them all over the ceiling and the windows. It was beautiful, if I do say so myself. I used this glittery paper that was thin, slippery, and a little hard to work with, but it was worth it."

I tried not to cringe at the thought of cutting out paper snowflakes. It sounded like just the kind of project I would try to find an excuse to escape.

"Don't you need me to run the pie shop? We've been pretty busy lately," I said. I felt proud of my valid excuse to avoid this task.

"Don't worry, your mother is coming, and we can all take turns serving people as they come in. The Morning Pie Crew is coming too. Flora has a project she thought we'd all enjoy too. I think it has something to do with folding paper flowers." I tried to hold in a groan. "But anyway, they'll be able to help while they're here too."

"Don't they have their own shops to run?" I asked. Now I was desperate to get out of this. Mr. Barnes was a yoga teacher, so I knew he had some free time depending on his schedule, but Lena ran the hardware store, and Flora owned the bookstore. Didn't people need to fix things and buy books this time of year?

"All their holiday employees are up to speed and can do without them for a few days. Plus, today's going to be quiet. Lots of people are getting ready for the snowman building contest tomorrow," she said. "Which reminds me, we probably need to practice a few more times."

Wow, this day just kept getting better and better.

Two hours later I could barely feel my fingers. Lena, Flora, Mr. Barnes, my mother, Aunt Erma, and I all crowded around two of the three at the front of the pie shop. Aunt Erma and I had prepped and set out all the pies for the day. Customers were wandering in here and there, and I always made sure I was the first one to leap out of my chair to serve them.

"Isn't there some magic way to do this?" I asked as I cut yet another disappointing snowflake. Aunt Erma kept assuring me that they were good.

"Every snowflake is supposed to be different, and yours sure are different," Lena said.

"Thanks," I said, glaring at her a little.

"You can't magic away everything," Aunt Erma said. "We aren't in a children's movie."

I sighed and folded another piece of paper. A customer walked in, and of course, I was the first one behind the counter. I took my time serving them. So much so that they began drumming their fingers on the counter. The nerve! Hadn't they ever heard of small town charm? Where the service is slow, but the people are friendly, and your mailman is also the barber?

"So, tell us about that fella I saw you with," Lena said during a lull in the conversation.

All eyes turned to me. There was no getting out of this now.

"Oh, you mean Josh?" I asked buying time, trying to figure out what I was going to tell them.

My mother's eyebrows shot up. "Josh was here?" She had speculated many times that Josh had feelings for me, and I had repeatedly reassured her that she was imagining things. The smug look on her face grated on me.

"He just came to say hi. He's working on a job nearby. I didn't get much of a chance to talk to him," I said.

We must have said his name too many times and summoned him. He walked through the door.

"Hi Josh," I said, trying to keep my tone calm, but it came out a little too high pitched. The whole table's eyes went from me to him and back to me again.

He froze for a second when he saw me at a table full of people. He quickly regained his composure.

"Hi, Susie. Hi, Mrs. Daniels," he said, nodding towards my mom. "Hi, everyone else. I didn't mean to interrupt. Maybe I can come back later." He backed towards the door so quickly he almost tripped over his own feet.

"Nonsense," Lena said pulling up another chair to our already crowded table. "There's plenty of room here, and we could really use some help cutting these snowflakes. I think Erma wants to fill the entire shop with them. There won't be room for customers, but who cares about the details, right?"

Aunt Erma rolled her eyes. "Oh, quit begin a drama queen, Lena. I'll share some of these with you."

"I run a hardware store. I can't have people getting distracted by all these sparkly snowflakes," she grumbled, but I saw her perk up a little.

Josh sat down on the corner of the chair, his hands folded tightly in his lap. He looked about as awkward as I felt. After five minutes though, he had Mr. Barnes showing him how to do the eagle pose and had Flora glowing when they discussed their favorite books, and he and Lena got into a heated discussion over which brand of drill was the best. That was how Josh was. He charmed everyone around him easily. I had always admired that skill. I had a way of alienating or making people uncomfortable with my failed jokes. He hadn't fully won over Aunt Erma yet though. She eyed him skeptically when he asked her about the best method for making pie crust. My mother was already in love with him, so he didn't have to bother with anything more than a little small chat with her. Sometimes I think my mother would rather have him as a child than me.

I was deep in thought about how I would explain this group date to Henry when I heard Josh say, "I'd love to come. Thank you so much for the invitation."

"You'd love to come where?" I asked.

"He's going to celebrate Christmas dinner with us," Flora said.

"What?" I asked. It came out sounding a little more harsh than I intended.

Just then, Henry walked through the door. "Henry," the room greeted him in chorus. I waved a crooked snowflake at him.

"You're pretty good at that," he pointed at my pile.

"Don't patronize me." I glared at him. He smiled innocently at me.

He noticed Josh and extended his hand. "I'm Henry."

Josh stood up and shook it, introducing himself.

"Josh is a friend of mine from back home," I said. I saw Henry's eyes quickly size up Josh, and I could feel the gaze of the group as they studied every nuance of our reactions.

"I should really get going," Josh said. "Thanks for letting me join in the fun." He puffed up his chest a little as he said goodbye to Henry. I got up to follow him out because we still needed to talk, but a large group walked through the door clamoring for pie.

"Can you help, Susie?" Aunt Erma asked sensing my hesitation about going after Josh. I sighed and turned back to the front counter to serve pie.

Later that night in the apartment, I was decorating the Christmas tree with my mom and Aunt Erma. As was to be expected, Aunt Erma had boxes and boxes of decorations. She was a little short on the tree though. The tree stood only about shoulder height to me.

41

"How are we going to fit all these decorations on that tiny thing?" my mother asked.

"Don't worry, they'll fit," Aunt Erma said. She disappeared into the kitchen.

"So, Josh is back," my mother said, unwrapping the first ornament. It was a Christmas fairy with a red sparkly dress and gold wings.

"Yes," I said. I focused all my attention on opening a box of silver and red shiny balls. I could feel my mother's eyes boring into me, but I kept my head down and examined the balls with more enthusiasm than I'd ever examined any balls before.
I screeched and threw the red ball I had been holding onto the ground. It shattered, and pieces flew across the wood floor. Mitzy came running over to see what was wrong.

"No Mitzy," I cried, picking her up so she didn't cut her paws on the sharp bits.

"What's wrong?" my mom asked. Aunt Erma rushed in from the kitchen.

"I saw. I saw…" I pointed to the broken pieces, clutching Mitzy so tightly she began to squirm in my arms. I couldn't say it out loud. It sounded absolutely insane.

"What did you see?" Aunt Erma asked. She put her arm around me and led me over to the sofa.

"I saw Brenda's face in the reflection of the ball," I said. Yup, it sounded crazy. "It had to be my imagination, right?" I looked to my mother and Aunt Erma for reassurance, but instead of giving it to me they were exchanging concerned glances. "That's not possible, right?" I asked again.

"It's possible," Aunt Erma said.

"But it's not good," my mom said.

"She was actually looking at me?" I asked. My voice was getting higher, almost reaching a hysterical pitch now. Mitzy finally squirmed her way out of my arms and onto the floor in

42

front of me. She gave me an indignant sigh before trotting off to her bed in the corner.

"I'm afraid so," Aunt Erma said. "It's a very powerful magic. It takes a lot of energy and a lot of special ingredients that I don't know where she would have gotten.   I'm worried she might have more help than we thought."

"Didn't you say that their son...what was his name? Flan? Dan?" my mother snapped her fingers.

"Stan," I said.

"Right," she said pointing at me. "Didn't you say that Stan was a delivery man? Wouldn't that mean he would have access to a lot of stuff?   Maybe he became a delivery man wherever they're living now. Or maybe he stocked up on stuff while he was traveling around town here. A delivery man gets a fair amount of access."

I remembered Stan looking in the cupboards of the kitchen when he was trying to find Aunt Erma's secret spices last month. I shuddered a little when I thought about how often he and I were in the kitchen alone.

"It's OK," Aunt Erma patting my arm. "She's gone now."

I went over to the boxes of balls and examined them all. The only face I saw was my own as I stared intently waiting for hers to appear.

"She's not there," my mother said.

"She probably focused all of her magic on that ball. Now that it's broken she won't have a way in for a while," Aunt Erma said.

I tried to believe her, but she let me put the boxes of baubles in the back of the closet, jamming them behind all the jackets and sweaters.

"Here, have some hot chocolate."   Aunt Erma disappeared into the kitchen and returned carrying a tray of red mugs full of steaming liquid. I took a mug and felt the heat on my hands. I inhaled the hot chocolate. The peppermint smell made my nose tingle. The first sip warmed me all the way to my toes.

"I put a little something in there," Aunt Erma said.

"A special spice?" I asked.

"No, a special Schnapps," she said.

Staring at the beautifully decorated Christmas tree just didn't give me the usual joy. Aunt Erma set the lights to sparkle in time to the Christmas music we had playing, but even that didn't make me feel better.

Chapter 6

Dear Elodie,

I have a very serious relationship problem. I've been with this guy for a few weeks, and it has been wonderful. He really is everything I could have ever wanted. My problem is that this other guy has come out of the woodwork and said he is in love with me too. I've been single for a long time. Where was this guy then? He had been around for years just twiddling his thumbs not saying anything, and then now when I'm happy and with someone new, he steps to center stage with some dramatic proclamation. I don't know what to do. He's not that great of a guy, but I don't want to hurt his feelings. How do I get him out of here and get back to my prince without hurting the other guy's feelings? I never thought I'd be in a love triangle, and when I did dream about it, I didn't imagine it would be so hard.

> *Sincerely,*
> *Everyone Loves Me*

Dear Everyone Loves Me,

Clearly you have to send the other guy packing as soon as possible. It sounds like you're with the right guy now. Why would the other guy choose this time to reveal his feelings? Some men always want what they can't have, and this seems like a classic case of that. I think you should tell him to go away and not come back. If he had really loved you, he would not have popped back into your life like this.

> *Ask and I'll answer,*
> *Elodie*

I stormed into the nursing home, barely acknowledging Lacey, the woman behind the front counter.

"Henry's in the dining room," she called.

"Thanks," I said over my shoulder, not slowing down. He was sitting at a table playing cards with a few of the residents.

"Can I talk to you?" I asked him through clenched teeth not even saying hi to the other people. They looked at him with raised eyebrows, and he looked a little sheepish.

"Sure," he said, slowly getting up. "I'll be right back. No peeking at my cards Mr. Gary," he said.

Mr. Gary gave him a wide-eyed innocent look through his thick rimmed glasses. "I'm no cheater," he said. "You're just a terrible player."

The table cracked up, and Henry followed me outside.

"I'm guessing you've read today's paper," he said ducking his head.

"Yup," I said, crossing my arms. "Care to explain, oh my royal prince." He grimaced.

"Yeah, I wrote that when I was upset. I probably should have waited and read it after I had calmed down before sending it to my editor," he said.

"Ya think?" I asked.

"You have to understand this is hard for me too," he said, rubbing his forehead.

"And that gives you the right to publish this?" I held up the newspaper. I wasn't ready to let him off the hook.

"No, you're right. I shouldn't have said it. I'm really sorry. I know you're actually going through a hard time, and I know Josh is too," he added reluctantly. "I just really like you."

"You think that's an excuse?" I asked.

"No, of course not," he said. "I made a mistake."

"Just please don't use my personal life in your column again," I said. His apologies were making my boiling anger cool to a simmer.

"Deal," he said, reaching out his hand. I shook it. "Unless it's something really juicy," he added. I gently punched his shoulder.

"I'm going to start writing a competing advice column," I said.

His eyes widened, "Never mind, I take it back. I'm sorry!" He carefully took the newspaper out of my hand. "Maybe I can hold onto this." He said, "So, you don't do anything crazy, like reread this garbage." I let him have it because he was probably right. If I read it again, I'd be angry again.

Well, I thought as I walked away and headed back to the pie shop. Henry and I had survived our first fight. And since I was the winner, I think it went well. I wondered if Henry would be able to keep his anonymity as Elodie with such a blatant letter. It was so obviously about me and Josh and Henry. Wouldn't everyone be able to see that?

It turns out it was easy for them to miss the signs. The Morning Pie Crew talked about Ask Elodie, as they usually did, but they didn't ever say anything about me and Henry. Were they being polite? I considered the possibility, but then I thought who am I kidding? The Morning Pie Crew never bothered to be polite or respect my privacy. After mine and Henry's fourth date, Lena wiggled her eyebrows at me and asked if Henry had "buttered my roll."

Aunt Erma and I were supposed to go out and get a Christmas tree for the front of the pie shop today while my mother kept things running in the shop. We had bought a tree after Thanksgiving, but someone, and I'm not naming names, had been learning magic and accidentally cast a spell last week that knocked all the needles off the tree. Now we needed a new one so people would stop asking where our tree was.

"I'm not going to be able to go tree shopping with you today," Aunt Erma said as I wrote the different pie flavors on the chalkboard.

I turned to her, trying to hide my disappointment. "Why not?"

"Violet wants me to strategize with her. There's been a little chatter that the IMPs are going to try something again soon," she said. As much as I had been looking forward to this outing today, I couldn't argue with that. "I ran into Henry when I was at the grocery store, and he offered to go with you," she said.

"Great," I said with a forced smile. I had forgiven Henry, but I thought I would have another day to fully cool off before we spent too much time together. Henry entered the shop before I could try and get out of it with a "maybe we can go tomorrow" suggestion.

"Hi," Henry greeted us. His smiled at me with a hint of guilt and a bit of hope.

I grabbed my coat and Aunt Erma sent us off with a reminder to get a small tree.

"There's not a lot of room here, so make sure you get one that's yay big or smaller," she held her hand up to her waist.

We walked the short distance to the tree lot that was set up in the parking lot by the church mostly in silence. Most people had already gotten their trees since it was mid-December. The lot had just a few near the front. The leftovers had wonky branches or crooked tops. No one was manning the booth. There was just a bucket hanging in front of it with a sign that said, "Pay here."

"They're all too big," I said, looking up at one that was missing half its needles. I'd be in big trouble if I brought that one back.

"I think there's more in the field back there," he said, disappearing behind the church. I slowly wandered after him. "Help," I heard Henry yell, and I ran towards the sound of his voice. I rounded the corner and saw Henry standing in an awkward position knee deep in snow. "Stop," he said when I got close.

"What's wrong?"

"The snow. I'm stuck." He moved a little and sunk down a few more inches. "It's sticky. I think there's a spell on it."

"Should I call Violet?" I asked. My heart was racing as Henry went down another inch.

Henry nodded, his face was pale. He closed his eyes, and I could hear him murmuring something. A spell or a prayer. I wasn't sure.

I gave Violet a slightly hysterical account of what was happening.

"I'll be there in three minutes," she said. I wasn't sure if Henry had three minutes. He was already waist deep.

"It's just so sticky," he said. He lifted his mittened hand up, and the snow clung to it, stringy, almost like molasses. I had an idea. Last week I had dropped a giant glass jug of maple syrup. The glass shattered, and syrup splattered everywhere. The puddle had spread quickly and seemed to cover every surface in the kitchen in no time, including my pants. I was just moaning about how much time it would take me to clean up all the syrup, when Aunt Erma taught me a spell that made the syrup not sticky. It was still a mess to clean up, but it was just liquid, so it had been so much easier.

I tried the spell now. I closed my eyes and focused all my energy towards Henry as I spoke the words Aunt Erma taught me. I snapped my eyes open, not really thinking I had accomplished anything, but there was Henry, waist deep in a puddle instead of the snow. I ran over and pulled him out of the puddle just as Violet and Aunt Erma appeared on the scene.

Aunt Erma ran over and threw her arms around me and Henry. "Are you two OK?" she asked, squeezing us tightly. We both nodded shakily, and told her and Violet what happened.

"I'm going to get some Magic Enforcement Officers out here to inspect the scene," Violet said. "Erma said she was supposed to be here. I think the IMPs were trying to catch her."

"I'm sorry you got caught in it." Aunt Erma looked like she might cry.

"You should get inside," Violet told Henry whose teeth were chattering. Aunt Erma ushered us back to the pie shop, and I brought Henry upstairs to find something he could change into. I gave him a pair of fleece pants and an oversized t-shirt that I wore as pajamas sometimes. I had gotten a little wet when I was pulling him out of the puddle, so I changed into a dry pair of fleece leggings and a red tunic sweatshirt.

When Henry came out of the bathroom, he came over to me and gently twisted one of my curls around his finger. "Thanks for saving my life," he said. His breath smelled minty fresh, and I had a feeling he'd just used some of my mouthwash. I was suddenly a little self conscious of my coffee breath.

"Anytime," I said out of the corner of my mouth so as not to blow my bad breath into his face. He leaned in and kissed me long and slow. His lips were still ice cold, but I didn't mind, and he didn't seem to mind my coffee breath.

"We should probably get back downstairs," he said.

I groaned and let my head fall to his chest. "We're going to be stuck answering questions forever," I said.

The whole Morning Pie Crew was at the front of the shop drinking coffee when we went back downstairs. I was right, their questions began the minute they saw us. We were about at the

50

part where Henry was sinking in the snow when Violet showed up.

"How did you get him out of there?" she asked in her direct way. I was a little miffed that she was ruining the dramatic tension I was building up in my story, but I told her the spell I used and why. Violet narrowed her eyes at me.

"The magic in the snow was very powerful," she said. "That spell shouldn't have worked on it."

I shrugged as everyone stared at me. "Maybe it was the adrenaline? Can that make magic stronger?" I asked.

"No," Violet said, still studying me. I shifted uncomfortably. "You just did a whole different level of magic."

I was relieved that night when Holly said she was still free to grab a drink at Sal's. I could really use a night out. I got there first, which wasn't unusual. Sal's was our one bar in town. It was dimly lit with creaky wooden floors. There was a jukebox in the front and a pool table in the back. I ordered a beer from Sal and sat near the pool table. Maybe this would be the night I discovered my super hidden talent for pool.I hummed along to the country Christmas songs that were playing from the jukebox and stared blankly at the football game that was on TV. I was almost finished with my first beer by the time Holly rushed in.

"Sorry I'm late," she said, patting her windblown blonde hair down. "Cabbage catastrophe." Holly worked at Basil's Market, and I'd gotten used to her strange food emergencies. She ordered a drink, something pink and fizzy, and we got right into the gossip.

"Two men vying for your love, that must be tough," she said. I let my head fall to the table with a groan.

"I don't know what to do," I said. "I don't want to hurt anyone's feelings."

"That's your problem," she said, "You have to stop worrying about their feelings and think about what you want."

51

"I want to learn how to windsurf," I said, thoughtfully tapping my chin.

"Fair enough," she said, and clinked her glass against mine.

By the time we were both working on our second drink, we were trying to solve the problem of the IMPs.

"What's their deal anyway?" I asked.

"There are some people who think that non-magical people should be hiding from us since we're supposedly the more powerful ones," she said. "Personally, I think they should just chill. Our life here is pretty great, and it could be really dangerous for magic to get out in the world."

"How long have they been around?"

"They've been around for a long time, but they haven't really been active for the last several years. Everyone thought they gave up. No one realized Alice was part of this bigger movement until the posters were plastered everywhere," she said, biting a cherry off the stem.

"How do we stop them?" I was ripping my cocktail napkin into tiny pieces. Holly gently took the napkin away from me and shrugged.

"We keep them from getting too much magic."

After that we moved on to solving more important problems, like whether or not Holly could catch the kernels of popcorn that I threw to her.

Chapter 7

Dear Elodie,

I think my house is haunted. I live alone and several times a week when I come home the remote control is in a different spot or a door is open that I'm sure I left closed. Whenever I buy a box of cookies, it always disappears within a couple days with nothing but a few crumbs on the bottom. It has to be ghosts, right? I tried putting up a camera so I could see them, but the camera always stops recording on the days when the ghost visits.

The only other person who has a key to my house is my neighbor. He said he's never seen anyone coming or going when I'm not home.

What should I do? Try to befriend the ghost in my house, or move?

Sincerely,
Victim of a Ghoulish Guest

Dear Victim of a Ghoulish Guest,

I would take the key back from your neighbor. If you don't believe me, hide a camera somewhere and don't tell your neighbor where it is. You just might see a face you recognize.

Ask and I''ll Answer,
Elodie

I woke up feeling unsettled the next morning. After seeing Brenda's face in the Christmas ornament a couple nights ago, and Henry almost getting eaten by a pile of snow yesterday, I was worried about what today might bring. I kept checking every reflective surface to see if a face other than my own was looking back at me. I got ready quickly so I didn't have to be alone in the bathroom with the mirror for too long, and I gave the Christmas tree wide berth.

Aunt Erma was already down in the kitchen prepping pies. No matter how early I got up, she always seemed to be up earlier. I wondered if she ever actually slept.

"How did you sleep?" she asked examining me. I shrugged. "I need your head in the game today."

Oh right, it was the day of the snowman building contest.

"The snow in the square is all packed down from everyone walking through and kids playing. How are they going to have enough for the contest?" I asked.

"They have snow making machines." Aunt Erma pulled her flour covered hands out of the bowl to do the air quotes she often used when she meant someone was going to use magic.

I helped Aunt Erma with the prep. If there was anyone who wasn't in the Christmas spirit yet, today's choices would certainly make them feel jolly. We had a peppermint cream pie, a Ho Ho hot chocolate cream, a Rudolph's nose cherry crumble, and an elf's apple ribbon pie. We set out all the pies and unlocked the door. Aunt Erma posted a sign at the front door that announced our shortened hours for the day, but of course everyone in town already knew about them. We were going to be closed during the competition, but we would reopen afterwards so everyone could come in for a slice of pie and a nice steaming cup of coffee or hot chocolate. We served the first few early bird customers, and then the shop emptied.

54

"Now sit, eat," Aunt Erma said pushing me towards a table with a slice of pie in her hand. "You need your energy for the competition."

"To be honest, my heart just isn't really in it," I said. I felt like I was going to be looking over my shoulder at every turn all day. I had already thought I'd seen Dennis and Brenda walk past the pie shop three times this morning. My skin prickled at the thought of being outside in the open surrounded by snow. Spells could just fly from any direction and sticky piles of magic snow could try to suck me in.

"It will be fine," Aunt Erma assured me. She set a cup of coffee in front of me.

"I don't know if I can handle any more coffee," I said. My leg was already jiggling under the table.

"Don't worry, it's decaf," she said. She put her hand on my knee and firmly held it down.

I was halfway through the slice of pie when my nerves began to settle.

"What's in this pie?" I asked, a little suspiciously.

"Oh, you know, a sprinkle of this, a dash of that," she said with a wink. "Enjoy every bite, and you'll be ready for the competition."

The creamy chocolate flavor was easy to devour. I drank the coffee, and by the time we had to go outside for the competition, I had almost forgotten that we were all in terrible danger.

I could see the clouds of my breath when we went outside. Mitzy came along dressed in her Erma's Pie Shop dog coat. The coat was sparkly and red, lined with white fur, and when Mitzy wore it, she lifted her paws high in a proud prance. It had taken a week, but I wasn't embarrassed to walk with her anymore when she was wearing it. Aunt Erma was in a bright red coat with green polka dots. She wore a large hat shaped like a snowman. It had to be at least two feet high. She carried red and green pom poms with her.

"Pom poms?" I asked trying to hide my smile.

"Yes, I'm not only the sponsor, I'm also the official cheerleader," she said with a wave of her pom poms.

I hoped she wasn't wearing a cheerleading uniform under that coat. With Aunt Erma, anything was possible.

The crowd had already begun to gather in the square. The snow was piled high. There were a couple fires burning in barrels at the edge, and people huddled around the flames holding their mittened hands out to warm them. Christmas music played from somewhere in the bundle of evergreen trees at the corner of the square. Somehow the place seemed to be covered in even more Christmas lights. The air practically sparkled with the excited energy that buzzed around. I half expected to see Santa Claus fly in on his sleigh.

Wait, there was Santa Claus — or at least Tanner O'Connell dressed up as Santa Claus. The crowd was eating it up as he walked around and took pictures with people. Several children and a few adults told him what they wanted for Christmas. Then he walked up to the steps of the gazebo. The gazebo was lined with lights that were flashing to the beat of the Christmas music that was playing. When he took the microphone and began to speak, the music died down. I don't know if it was the outfit or magic, but his voice sounded two octaves deeper than it did most days.

"Welcome to the 56th Annual Snowman Building Contest! This has been a proud tradition for Hocus Hills thanks to our former mayor Barney Wallace who created this competition one drunken night," Tanner said. Barney was in his eighties now and sat covered in a blanket on a bench in the gazebo. He waved proudly to the crowd. "Every year the competition gets fiercer, and the prize gets better." He held up a large green gift bag. "I don't want to ruin the surprise, but trust me, there are some spectacular goodies in here." I thought he was overselling it a bit since I had helped Aunt Erma put together the grand prize. It was a dozen mini pumpkin pies, a Hocus Hills t-shirt, and a mug that said, "I built the best snowman" on one side and "Hocus Hills 56th Annual Snowman Building Contest proudly sponsored by Erma's Pie Shop" on the other side. He went on to thank Erma's Pie Shop and then rambled on for another ten minutes about what a proud tradition this was for our town. I stopped listening and started planning what I wanted for lunch. I was leaning towards a grilled cheese sandwich and tomato soup. As he began to wind down, Aunt Erma grabbed my arm.

"You have to focus. Get your head in the game. Remember everything we practiced," she said. "Round balls. Make the first one large, then make the head second, and make the third one the middle so you can make it exactly the right size. You know when you make the middle second then the proportions get all off."

"I know. I remember," I said as I eyed a passersby's steaming paper cup of hot chocolate longingly. I was as competitive as the next person. Some people, such as Josh, might say I was even more competitive than the average person. All because of one out of hand Pictionary incident in which I pulled all the cards out of the box and threw them at Josh. It was a surprisingly satisfying experience. Josh had just stared at me with wide eyes and then burst out laughing. I couldn't help it. I ended up laughing too. But since I couldn't win this, it didn't seem like it was worth all the determination Aunt Erma was pouring into it.

"Get ready," Santa Claus yelled into the microphone. It was so loud I cringed and plugged the ear that was closest to the speakers. "Get set." People shuffled into the places nearest the large snow piles. Then we all froze. The only sound was the wind and the occasional shuffle of people's jackets.

"Gooooooooo," he yelled, and everyone sprang into action. I wanted to watch the mayhem, but Aunt Erma was yelling at me. I reluctantly gathered some snow in my hands to get the first ball going.

"Come on. Get rolling. Make the edges smooth," she commanded. "Susie," she snapped her fingers at me, and I looked at her. "You have to go faster," she said. I looked around and saw that everyone else was much further along than I was, but they also seemed to be having a lot more fun than I was.

"Isn't there some rule about not talking to the snowman makers?" I asked.

"Nope," Aunt Erma replied, not missing a beat.

"Hey, you're here," Henry rushed over to me.

"Don't distract her, Henry," Aunt Erma scolded. Aunt Erma was holding a bag full of our props for the snowman. She even included a pie tin that I was supposed to use positioned in the snowman's arms. "You have to make sure it's at a jaunty angle and that it doesn't fall. That would be horrible if it fell," Aunt Erma had told me one day last week when we were practicing. I had broken three glass pie plates before Aunt Erma decided we should just use an aluminum tin full of whipped cream. "It doesn't look as pretty as the glass ones, but all of the judges will be looking at the whipped cream anyway. Oh, especially if we add chocolate chips," she congratulated herself with her great idea. Then she pulled out the notebook and made a note. She had been doing that all along, making notes for me to study later.

"How are you doing?" Henry asked in a low voice. Aunt Erma and her superhuman hearing narrowed her eyes at him.

"Great," I said. "Building a snowman is fun." I gave him a big fake smile and an overly enthusiastic thumbs up. He laughed.

"Violet sent me to talk to both of you, actually," he said.

Aunt Erma let out a dramatic sigh. "OK, what is it?" she asked.

"Violet said there have been some indications that the Stan has been in town," he said.

"In this town?" I felt my heart begin to beat faster. Stan seemed harmless enough, albeit a bit of a bumbling buffoon when I met him last month, but it turned out he was in on a plot to take over our town.

He nodded.

Aunt Erma's brow furrowed. "Does she know why? What is he trying to do?"

"She's not sure. She's trying to figure that out now. She said she just caught the faintest traces of his magic. One of the other officers picked it up, but he must have used a very good magic eraser because it disappeared quickly," he said.

"Are there any other IMPs here?" I asked.

"Not that we know of," he said.

"We'll keep our antennas up," Aunt Erma assured him.

"Good," Henry said. "I'm going to stay here and help for a while. Just to make sure nothing happens."

The adrenaline was pumping through my veins after Henry's very troubling announcement. I worked quickly, packing the snow tighter on my snowman. The thought of Stan back in town sent goosebumps up and down my arms. Aunt Erma seemed pleased with my new work ethic, ignoring the fact that it was happening out of fear.

"Don't worry," she said. "The whole town is here. They wouldn't dare try anything today. Too many magical people around," she said the last part in a low voice. There were a lot of tourists who came for the contest.

I dressed the snowman in an apron and managed to put the whipped cream pie on the stick arm perfectly. OK, maybe it took me a few tries, but still, it seemed to stay. And more importantly, Aunt Erma seemed happy. Henry helped me stick the two poles in the ground behind the snowman. Stretched between them was a banner that read, "Erma's Pies, stop by for a slice after the competition. All entrants will receive ten percent off a slice of pie."

I looked around and marveled at the artistry of the other creations. I had never before realized that snowmen could be more than just three balls with some coal eyes and a carrot nose. These were amazing. "Frosty the Snowman" began to play from the speakers indicating the end of the competition, and Aunt Erma started singing along. Henry joined her and soon all the people surrounding us were singing. I tried to sing too, but I had a lump at the back of my throat. It happened every time a group of people sang together. There was something special about a group of people singing together that made me emotional. It really brought people together. We were a community of people. All a little strange, but all of us were doing this same crazy project. Even the tourists were part of our beautiful small town of Hocus Hills on a day like today. I felt my desire to stay strengthen.

I jumped when I felt something poke me. I turned, expecting to see Henry, but it was the arm of the snowman tapping my shoulder. Was Aunt Erma using magic on the snowman? I thought they said they waited until after all the tourists had left to do that kind of magic. I looked over at Aunt Erma to see what the heck was going on. The look on her face made it clear she wasn't doing it. Then everything went white as the snowman hurled the tin of whipped cream at my face.

I could hear the commotion begin around me. People yelling. Lots of alarmed voices crying out, "What's happening?" I frantically wiped the whipped cream away from my face. When I had finally cleared the cream away from my eyes, I saw Aunt Erma and Henry trying to cast spells in the direction of the snowmen, but they didn't seem to stop them. Henry was right next to me. His hand on my back.

"Are you OK?" he asked. His eyes were filled with worry.

"Fine," I said.

A woman's voice came on over the speaker singing loudly to the Christmas music. Was that Brenda's voice? "Tired of keeping your magic hidden? Being yourself has always been forbidden? Join a great cause. Let's lighten the laws. It's time we see Improvement for Magical People!"

Most of the snowmen across the square were just dancing to the music. It was only the ones near us that seemed to be trying to attack. They would roll aggressively towards us and Aunt Erma or Henry would cast a spell, and they would roll backwards only to come at us again a minute later. The square had cleared of all non-magical people. I wondered how this would be explained to them. As someone who was still pretty new to this magic thing, I completely understood their panic. Several town residents were there trying to help stop the mayhem. The annoying song about joining the IMPs was playing on repeat over the speaker.

"What can I do?" I asked. "Teach me the spell."

"You need to stay out of this," Erma added in a low voice. I opened my mouth to protest, but she gave me such a sharp look that I closed it again.

Mr. Barnes, Lena, and Flora rushed over. Along the way, Mr. Barnes had to dodge a rolling snowman whose thrashing stick arms came within inches of his face.

"We have to stop the madness," Flora said. Her eyes were wide.

"Let's all cast a protective spell around us," Aunt Erma said. "They only seem to be coming after our group."

61

"What happened to you?" Lena asked, sizing up my whipped cream covered front. "Never mind, tell us later." She cut me off before I could even get a word out. "What spell are we going to use?"

"The usual ones aren't working," Flora said.

As they debated about which spell would work, a snowman dressed like a witch was coming towards me waving its broom. The protective spell must be wearing off.

"Hey, guys?" I said, shrinking back. Henry looked up and saw it. He cast a spell, and it began to back up. I had an idea and lunged for the broom.

"What are you doing?" he yelled, sounding shocked and panicked.

I was too busy wrestling the broom away from the snowman to answer. We were rolling on the ground. I gripped the handle tightly with both hands as I tried to kick the icy round balls off me. I came away triumphantly with just a few scratches and the broom in my hands.

"They're just a bunch of snowflakes," I said, recognizing the irony considering how Henry was almost killed by a bunch of snowflakes yesterday. Then I lifted the broom above my head and swung it down on the snowman, turning it back into a pile of snow.

The others got on board quickly, using anything they could find to smash the snowmen. Tanner was using the bag of presents that was part of his Santa costume to bludgeon a snowman who looked like a cartoon bear. Lena had found a plastic sword and was taking out snowmen while yelling, "On guard. Take that, and that, and that," with every swing.

In no time, all the snowmen had been reduced to piles of snow, and the square was littered with props. In the chaos, someone had smashed the speakers and the singing had stopped.

It was silent for a moment. I couldn't hear anything but my heavy breathing.

"Well everyone," Violet stood on the steps of the gazebo. I'm not even sure when she got there. "That was more excitement than we bargained for today." She was trying to keep her tone light. "Thank you all for your hard work here. The IMPs have been acting out, but we have it under control."

"This didn't look like it was under control," someone from the crowd yelled.

"There were a lot of outsiders here today. What are you going to do about that?" another voice called.

"We're sending some teams out to take care of that," Violet said calmly.

"I think some of them have left already," someone said.

"Can you blame them?" another voice added. "They just saw a whole passel of snowmen come to life."

"We're going to take care of them too," Violet said. "By tomorrow, they will all think they've just had a very strange dream." This seemed to be a pattern, and I began to wonder how many of my strange dreams had actually happened. Had I once really fallen out of a boat and been rescued by a mermaid, or was that just a dream? I tried to make a mental note to ask Aunt Erma that very question next time we had a chance to talk. "As for right now, everyone should just go home and be with your families," Violet continued. "Keep your eyes and ears open, and report anything strange you might see to the Magical Enforcers immediately."

The crowd dispersed, and I followed the Morning Pie Crew, Aunt Erma, and Henry back to the pie shop. We all sank into chairs, except for Aunt Erma who went to turn up the heat and bring down dry socks for everyone. Mitzy followed her downstairs, eager to cheer up the exhausted crowd with her wagging tail.

Henry put his arm on my shoulder. "I hate to leave you right now, but I'm supposed to help the residents decorate for Christmas, and I have to stop at home to let Willy out first."

"Go, go," Aunt Erma said. "We're fine here." I tried to force a smile to show him, yes, of course we were fine. Aunt Erma said it, so it must be true.

He studied my face for a second and hesitated as though he knew what I was feeling. "I'll check in with you later," he said, giving my shoulder a squeeze.

He left and we all sat in silence for a minute. Aunt Erma's eyes had drifted closed. Then they snapped open.

"Aren't you supposed to go help him?" she asked.

"Well, yes, but," I began.

"But nothing," she said. "Everything is just fine here. You go and help string up those lights."

I felt torn. I loved decorating for Christmas, and I loved the enthusiasm and complete lack of boundaries that most people in the nursing home had, but there was anxiety in the pit of my stomach at the thought of leaving Aunt Erma alone. It was dangerous. Even I knew it was bad that the IMPs had hit right here in town.

"You go. You can all go," Aunt Erma insisted. "I've got my guard dog." Right on cue, Mitzy let out a cheerful yip. "I'm ready to have a quiet night in and try out some new pie recipes."

"OK, I said hesitantly. "I'll just go upstairs and change."

"I can walk you there," Mr. Barnes offered.

"I'll be fine," I said, trying to adopt Aunt Erma's bravado. "It's like a three block walk. I'll be there in no time."

"OK," he said, still looking a little unsure, but he left.

The rest of the Morning Pie Crew reluctantly stood.

"Are you sure you don't want me to say?" Flora asked. Aunt Erma turned her down, but that didn't stop her from asking three more times before Aunt Erma ushered her to the door.

I went upstairs to put on a drier outfit. I settled on a bright red tunic with black leggings. It was both Christmassy and allowed me to move in case I needed to tackle any other rogue snowmen.

"Keep an eye on Aunt Erma," I told Mitzy. She wagged her tail at me.

"Bye, Aunt Erma," I called as I headed towards the back door. She appeared from the front of the shop. "I'll be back soon," I told her.

"Pish posh," she dismissed me with a wave. "You stay out as long as you want. You kids have fun with all those old fogies." I gave her a hug and was out the door. I kept my eyes peeled for any stray snowmen who might roll into my path and attack at any moment.

Chapter 8

Despite my bravado when talking to Mr. Barnes, it was the longest three block walk I've ever had. Even the sound of the wind rustling through the trees was enough to make the hair on my arms stand at attention. The streets were deserted after the earlier fiasco which only added to my uneasiness.

So when my phone rang, I yelped and then tried to cover it with a cough, even though no one was around to hear me. It wasn't a number I recognized. I slid the button and answered.

"Susie Daniels?" a gruff voice asked.

"This is she," I said cautiously. I kicked myself for answering what sounded like it was going to be a sales call.

"This is Buster Hopkins from Top-Notch Construction." I stood up a little straighter. He was one of the big wigs in the construction scene in the city. "I hear you left Hal's."

That was one way of putting it. Hal had fired me when I took some time off to come help Aunt Erma at the pie shop.

"I want to offer you a job," he said. "I've seen some of your work, and I really admire your craftsmanship." He told me what my starting salary would be, and my mouth fell open. "Everyone I've talked to has great things to say about you. Well, everyone except Hal, but he's a bitter old fusspot, isn't he? So what do you say?"

"Can I think about it?" I asked. I was standing outside the nursing home now. I traced the gold letters on the sign out front that read, "Enchanted Woods," briefly forgetting my fear of rogue snowmen.

"Sure, we'll talk soon," he said and hung up.

As I walked towards the door, I shivered with excitement and anxiety. This job offer was a big deal, but was I ready to leave the life I had just started in Hocus Hills?

All of my concerns melted away though the moment I stepped inside. The warmth washed over me. I could hear voices singing "Rockin' Round the Christmas Tree." By the time I got back to the dining room, the smell of food brought my blood pressure down to a reasonable level and reminded me how incredibly hungry I was.

I peeked through the door. Henry was playing the piano and everyone was singing. Three couples were dancing around the Christmas tree. I held my breath as Mrs. Johnson dipped Mrs. Pappas, but despite their frail appearance, they performed the maneuver flawlessly.

"Susie, come and dance," Henry called out over the noise. Frank, a man whose large glasses accentuated his twinkling blue eyes, stretched his hand out towards me. I took it, and he spun me around all while singing every word. The song ended, and he gave me a gentlemanly bow as I thanked him for the dance.

"Looks like you guys waited for me to get started on the decorating," I said, looking at all the unopened boxes on the floor around the room.

Henry shrugged, "We may have gotten a little distracted."

"Last year it took us three weeks to get the Christmas decorations up because we kept getting distracted with sing-a-longs," Frank grinned.

"And dance-alongs," Claire Sprinkles added approaching us with a little sashay.

"Maybe we can get one box done today," I said going to the nearest box and opening it. It was full of a tangle of Christmas lights. "Who put these away?" I asked, pulling out the giant mess. "Is there magic to untangle these?"

They laughed. "No, we usually let the newest member of the Christmas decorating team take care of that," someone said.

"So it's my job, huh?" I said. I couldn't even see an end. "I think it looks good like this." I brought it over to an outlet and plugged it in. The lights were almost blinding, but beautiful. I decided it was probably too much of a fire hazard to leave like that. "I'll work on this." I sat on the floor with the ball in my lap. I was eager to take a job that didn't include hanging shiny Christmas baubles. I didn't want to risk seeing a face other than my own peering back at me. I shivered.

"Are you cold?" Henry asked, coming up behind me.

I looked at him incredulously. "Is it possible to be cold in this place?" I asked. They kept it so warm in here, I often fantasized about jumping in the snow to make snow angels when I stayed here for longer than ten minutes. "It's nothing," I said, forcing a smile. When he looked at me harder with his intense gaze, the one I was learning to both love and hate. I said, "I'll tell you more later."

"Here," he set down a plate piled with fluffy mashed potatoes. "I thought you might be hungry."

I threw my arms around him. "Thank you."

He looked a little taken aback. "You're welcome." He squeezed me tightly.

"Now that's how you know a couple is going to last," Frank said from his perch by the dessert table. "They show their appreciation for the small things."

I smiled at him, but felt knots in my stomach.

"I can help you with this," Henry said, pointing to the giant mess.

"No, this is all mine. I want all the glory when it's all done," I said. I had finally found an end and began to unwind it through the mess. "I do, however, want to be here when the

68

Christmas lights are put away this year. I will carefully wind them up," I said.

"I wound them up last year. . . carefully," Claire Sprinkles spoke up indignantly.

"You didn't carefully wind them up," Bernie Clausen said. "You drank a gallon of spiked eggnog and then wound them around your body and sang about being the light of our lives."

She paused for a second, not looking the slightest bit sheepish. "Oh yeah, that's right," then she burst into laughter. "Maybe you'd better come back and put them away. I still really love the eggnog."

I tried to focus on the project in front of me, but it was wonderfully distracting to be among this much positive energy. People were hanging Christmas decorations on the tree, pulling them out of boxes and laughing with stories about who bought them and what they represented.

Claire Sprinkles told a wildly inappropriate story about the "special fella" who bought her the ornament shaped like a bottle of champagne. I hummed along to the Christmas music playing in the background, and every now and then Henry would stop by to see how it was going. I was making headway, but it was a slow process. He was generally too busy trying to keep Mr. Leonard from climbing up on a chair to put the ornaments on top of the tree.

"No, Mr. Leonard," he would call. "You can reach the top of the tree from the ground." He would rush over and grab him just as he was about to make the step up onto the chair. Apparently Mr. Leonard had fallen off a chair last year and broken a hip. Climbing chairs was the least of his daring adventures though. Henry said sometimes he goes out at night, finds a sled, and tries to get up on the roof to slide off of it.

"He used to be a bobsledder. Almost made it to the Olympics too," Henry said. Henry was arranging a special bobsled experience for Mr. Leonard this winter. Apparently, there was a track less than an hour away, and Henry had rented a bus to take all the residents there. They were going to cheer on Mr. Leonard as he and a few other bobsledders made the journey down the hill.

"I just hope he makes it until that day," Henry said, rushing off to stop him from using the sofa as a trampoline to jump to the tree with an ornament in his hand.

I texted Aunt Erma to make sure she was doing OK. She responded, "Everything's peachy here, including the pie," and sent a picture of a peach pie. She told me she wanted to use some of the peaches she had canned last summer to bring a bit of warmth to this freezing weather. A minute later, another text came in. "Now stop bothering me and drink some eggnog." I smiled.

Two hours later, and I had successfully untangled the mess of lights. The whole room applauded and then helped me hang them. They filled the room with a colorful warm glow, and for the first time this year, I felt giddy for the upcoming holidays. I briefly wondered what I could get Henry. Clearly Henry was a very thoughtful gift giver. Just look at what he was going to do for Mr. Leonard. I was generally the buy him a sweater type, but clearly I was going to have to step up my game now.

"I should probably get back to Aunt Erma now," I said after we all enjoyed mugs of hot chocolate and there were a few more Christmas songs sung.

"I'll walk you out in just a second," Henry said. Then he began singing, "Silent Night." The whole room chimed in, and Henry followed me out to the front of the nursing home.

"Aren't you worried about leaving them alone right now? Mr. Leonard keeps eyeing that sofa," I said.

"They'll go to sleep as soon as they sing this song," he said. "It works every time." Then he yawned. "I might go to sleep after this song too."

We got to the front door and Henry leaned down to give me a kiss. I felt the tingling in my fingertips like I always did. Then I wondered at what point should I talk to him about Josh. I still felt like I should wait until I knew exactly what to say before I brought it up. Plus I was a big chicken who didn't want to ruin the lovely evening we'd had, so I said goodnight and left.

Giant snowflakes were falling gently from the sky. I jogged back to the pie shop — just because it was cold I told my ego, not because I was afraid anymore. I ran down the alley and let myself in the back door because I didn't want to see a reflection in the windows at the front of the shop. I had myself so worked up by the time I got there that I was pretty sure I would see Brenda's face even if she wasn't there.

I flew through the door and slammed it behind me, locking it quickly as though that could keep the bad magic out. I closed my eyes and took a deep breath letting the warmth at the back of the kitchen wash over me.

My eyes flew open when I heard a clutter right in front of me. Aunt Erma was in the kitchen pulling things out of the cupboard and throwing them on the kitchen island. She didn't even look over at me.

"Hi Aunt Erma," I said. She pulled out a handful of mixing spoons from a drawer and set them on the counter. "Did everything go OK while I was gone?" She walked around the island, grabbed a pie tin, and wandered back to the cupboard to put it away. "Aunt Erma," I said again. She still didn't even look my way. She just walked over to the handful of spoons and put them back in the drawer.

"Is everything OK?" I asked louder even though she wasn't that far away from me. She took the bottle of soap that was by the sink and set it on her desk at the back of the kitchen. As she turned and headed for the pantry, I grabbed her arm. Something was definitely off about the way she squinted at me.

"I'm going to call 911," I said.

"Sometimes I hide the last slice of blueberry pie and tell customers we're sold out, so I can eat it," she announced and then wrenched her arm out of my grip as she headed back towards the pantry. This didn't seem like a medical emergency anymore. This seemed like magic.

Chapter 9

"Was anyone here?" I asked her. She began to hum, "Let it Snow."

I pulled out my phone and called Flora first because she was the closest. Then I called Violet and my mother. Flora was at the door before I even finished the conversation with my mother. Aunt Erma was still wandering around the kitchen moving things in and out of cupboards and drawers. I had a feeling we wouldn't be able to find anything by the time she was done undoing her very carefully organized system.

Flora stood and observed for a minute. Then she slowly approached Aunt Erma as though she was afraid she would spook her. She spoke some words I couldn't understand. I assumed she was trying a spell. Aunt Erma paused for a minute and then kept puttering around. Flora hurried around the island so that she was standing in front of her again and murmured some more words. I stood in the corner of the kitchen. I wasn't sure I could help, so I was just trying not to get in the way.

"I don't care for that new haircut," Aunt Erma said before brushing past Flora to open the drawer with all the measuring cups. She grabbed one pile of red measuring cups and one pile of green and mixed them up, stacking them so they alternated colors.

My mom rushed in a few minutes later. She was wearing her sleek black coat over her yellow floral nightgown. Behind her, the snow fell off her in a trail of flakes.

"What is it?" she asked. "Erma, what's wrong?"

Aunt Erma handed my mom a handful of forks and said, "You have boney elbows." My mother looked at me wide-eyed, and I shrugged.

"She was like this when I came home," I said.

73

"Do you have any idea what it is?" my mother asked Flora.

"It looks like a truth spell gone wrong," Flora said. "I think we can guess who the culprits are."

My mother and Flora were talking at the other end of the kitchen, and I went over to Aunt Erma where she was crouched down pulling everything out from under the sink. I bent down next to her and took out a bottle of cleaner.

"Aunt Erma, did you tell them anything?" I asked in a low voice, thinking of the magic tree.

"Yes," Aunt Erma nodded solemnly. Her earnest eyes stared into mine for a moment. "I told them that I love pickles." I let out the breath I was holding. I stood up and took a few steps back to lean against kitchen island.

Violet arrived. It felt like we were all getting together far too often to do things other than celebrate Christmas. She went straight to Aunt Erma without saying a word. She murmured some words, but they didn't seem to have any more affect than Flora's did.

"Why is she rearranging the kitchen?" I asked. We all watched Aunt Erma cross the kitchen with a stack of plates.

"She's very strong," Violet said. "Most people on the receiving end of this spell would spill every secret they ever had. She's fighting the magic."

"Why didn't they take her with them?" I asked.

"They probably couldn't. Not with the protection spells she has on this place," Violet said. "I honestly don't know how they got to her at all. I can't seem to undo whatever spell they used."

"Fairy dust," my mother cried out, making me jump so high I knocked the handful of forks off the counter.

Everyone turned towards her, except Aunt Erma who pulled a handful of flour out of a bag. My mother was digging in

74

her purse without further explanation. She produced a bottle of sparkling dust. It was a small bottle very similar to the one I had used a few weeks ago to turn Aunt Erma back into a human after being a cat.

"Here," she waved it around wildly.

"That might work," Flora said, cautiously.

"Do you know the right spell," Violet asked.

My mother glared at her, and Violet held her hands up in mock surrender. I was just glad I wasn't on the receiving end of that look.

My mother walked closer to Aunt Erma. "Erma," she said, "Erma?"

Aunt Erma tilted her head to the side. "I put Susie's Christmas present under my bed," she said.

My mother poured a bit of the fairy dust onto the palm of her hand. Just as she was about to sprinkle it over Aunt Erma's head, Aunt Erma backed away and headed for the pantry.

"I'm going to need some help here," my mother said. We all moved in to help keep Aunt Erma still. She looked at me. I tried to smile, but it felt shaky.

"Keep the dog from the tree," she said to me.

Everyone turned towards me. "What does that mean?" Violet asked.

I shrugged because I really didn't know. I assumed she was talking about her super secret magic tree, but I didn't know what the dog stuff was about. Mitzy was upstairs. Maybe she was trying to tell me she needed the magic from the tree.

My mother was saying the spell and sprinkling the dust. After she was done, Aunt Erma looked at her for a minute. We all stood back and held our breaths.

"I took your Sally Sparkles doll when we were kids," Aunt Erma said to my mom. Then she scooted past Violet and to the pantry.

75

"What about the spices?" I asked.

"We could try them," Flora said, "but I'm not sure how much they would do since all the other magic isn't working."

I went to the fridge and pulled out every kind of pie we had in there. I didn't bother with slicing, I just stuck a fork in each one and scooped out a bite. The first one was apple. I held the bite in front of Aunt Erma's mouth, but she sidestepped it. I swirled it through the air like an airplane. I didn't realize how crazy I looked until I saw the expressions on everyone's face around me.

"Aunt Erma, please take a bite," I tried instead.

"OK," she said, and took the bite in her mouth. I did that with the remaining pies. At the end, she didn't seem any better.

"What do we do now?" I asked. I assumed someone else had another plan, but everyone exchanged hopeless glances.

"I'll go do some more research. If I can figure out exactly what spell was used and how it went wrong, then maybe we can undo it," Violet said.

"Maybe it will wear off soon too," I suggested. All of Aunt Erma's spices only worked for short periods of time. I assumed this would be temporary too.

"Yeah, maybe," Flora said in a voice that adults used when they told children that, "yeah, maybe," Santa would show up for dinner.

Violet and Flora left, and my mother and I brought Aunt Erma upstairs. Mitzy was waiting by the door as usual. She ran towards Aunt Erma then stopped in her tracks and backed away.

"It's OK, Mitzy," I said, but she just whined.

"Come on, Erma. Let's watch some television," my mom said. We led Aunt Erma over to the sofa, which doubled as my bed. She sat down and stared at the blank screen. I turned it on and flipped through the channels until I found a mindless sitcom.

I didn't think we needed a crime drama or something as horrific as the news on a night like tonight.

Mitzy walked in circles around the room, whining. Her tail was tucked between her legs.

"You should take Mitzy on a walk," my mother said. "I'll stay here with Erma."

I agreed grabbing my coat and Mitzy's leash. Usually that was enough to initiate an enthusiastic response, but Mitzy just kept circling. I tried asking her if she wanted to go on a walk, but still she didn't dance around my feet like she usually did. Finally, I went over to her and clipped the leash to her collar and led her out the door. She followed slowly with her head down.

"It's OK, Mitz," I told her softly on our way down the stairs. "We'll get her back."

The snow was still falling in fluffy flakes as we walked through the streets of the town. I tried to take a moment to enjoy the mixture of snow and Christmas lights, but my anxious thoughts kept interrupting. What if we never broke the spell? What if the IMPs discovered the magic tree? Had Aunt Erma given them any clues? Could the tree break the spell? How could I find the tree again? If Aunt Erma thought that I could just go out and find it again after seeing it once, she vastly overestimated my memory, but I vowed to try anyway.

Mitzy walked slowly alongside me. She didn't stop to sniff every light pole and tree like she usually did, which made me feel more unsettled. Of all the times I had wanted her to behave, now I wanted her to act like her normal spazzy self. I took her all the way around the square. I was hoping she would perk up, and I wanted to survey the scene of the earlier insanity. Someone had cleaned up quite well. All of the props were gone and the snow had been smoothed out so no one could tell it had been the site of a major snowman massacre. The Christmas lights twinkled brightly, happy to keep the secret. The only evidence left from the contest was a carrot stuck way up in a pine tree. We turned the last corner of the square and were going to head back to the pie shop, when Mitzy made an abrupt turn down a side street.

"No, Mitzy, this way," I said. I gently tugged at her leash, but she stood at attention and pointed her paw down the road. That was another new behavior. I weighed my options and followed her. It occurred to me that she was under some sort of spell too and that I was being led into a trap. "Mitzy, are you leading me into a trap?" I asked. I decided a couple weeks ago that talking to dogs was, in fact, acceptable behavior. Especially when the dog seemed to understand every word that you said.

She pulled at the leash again and I followed. We approached the yoga studio, and I heard a loud clatter come from inside. Mitzy pulled the leash, and I hurried towards the front door. I hesitated when I heard the sound of breaking glass. Mitzy pulled harder at her leash. She began to growl, and I tried to shush her. What should I do? Call Violet? Go inside and see what was happening? I debated.

"You thieving son of a . . .," I heard Mr. Barnes voice inside. The time for debating was over. Mitzy and I rushed through the front door of the yoga studio. There were only a few candles lit providing a flickering light. I felt the walls trying to find a light switch, but I couldn't find one.

"Mr. Barnes, are you OK?" I called. There was another crash. Mitzy tugged at her leash growling and barking with the ferocity of a much bigger dog. "Mr. Barnes?" I called again. I felt something rush past me, and I tried to grab it. My fingers caught a corner of cloth, and I held on tightly, but the cloth quickly went limp. Light filled the shop, and I had to squint against the brightness to see. Mr. Barnes stood at the corner of the room by a light switch. He had his hands on his knees, and he was breathing hard. I looked down at my hands. I was clutching a gray jacket. Mitzy had her teeth sunk into the other corner of the fabric. She had a look of determination in her eyes, but when she saw there was no one wearing it anymore, she let it go. I recognized the jacket. It was Stan's. I let it slide out of my fingers and into a pile on the ground.

"What happened?" I asked. My heart was still racing.

"Someone was in here," Mr. Barnes paused to take a deep cleansing yoga breath. "They stole from me." He waved his arm around as though he was going to say more, but he didn't.

"It was Stan," I pointed to the jacket. "I'll call Violet." I had her on speed dial now. Violet appeared quickly. Was she always in her business suit, ready to go?

Mr. Barnes said that he went to the diner to grab a bite to eat. When he came back he just lit a few candles and didn't turn on any lights because he was trying to relax. He had just started doing his nightly yoga exercises when he heard something. He headed towards the light switch, but someone bumped into him. He tried to grab the person, and there was a struggle. Apparently, some spells were thrown back and forth. Violet and Mr. Barnes referenced some spells that I hadn't learned about yet.

"He took my carving," Mr. Barnes pointed to a shelf on the wall where he'd had a carving of a gnome doing the splits. I had noticed it in the yoga classes I had taken with him. Mr. Barnes said it was supposed to provide inspiration, but I thought the smiling gnome mocked my inflexibility every time I tried to touch my toes.

"Why would he do that?" I asked. It seemed like a lot of trouble to go through for a gnome.

"Erma gave it to me," he said.

"It had some of her magic in it," Violet explained when she saw I still didn't understand.

"She gave it to me to protect my studio and promote calm within these walls." He was still looking at the empty shelf. My eyes widened as I wondered if it was carved out of wood from the magic tree.

"We'll find it," Violet put her hand on Mr. Barnes's shoulder in a rare display of affection. "I'll let you know when I know something." And with that, she was out the door.

I left a few minutes later after making sure that Mr. Barnes was alright. "I'm fine. It's nothing a little herbal tea won't fix," he said.

When I stepped outside, the snow was deep with the flakes falling so fast and thick that I knew I would never be able to make it to the magic tree in these conditions. I would have to try tomorrow.

Maybe Aunt Erma will be better by tomorrow, I thought hopefully.

Chapter 10

Dear Elodie,

Last Christmas, my mother gave me a necklace that had belonged to her mother and her mother's mother, all the way back to my great-great-great-grandmother. It was a beautiful gold pendant with stars and a tree engraved on it. I was thrilled when I received this family heirloom. My mother always said I couldn't be trusted with nice things, and when she presented the gift, she warned me to be very careful with it because if I lost it, the ghost of my great-great-great-grandmother would come back and curse me.

You can probably see where this is going. I wore it to an event the other night because it went so perfectly with my outfit and I'm a firm believer in not letting things just sit in a drawer and collect dust. I was on my way home when I realized it wasn't around my neck anymore. I looked everywhere in the car and even went back to the venue and searched on my hands and knees. The staff there tried to help, but no one found it.

Now I'm not sleeping and feel sick with worry. Worry over telling my mom. Worry that my great-great-great-grandmother will come back and curse me, and worry that I really can't be trusted with nice things.

Do you know any tricks for locating something that's lost? How do I get over this guilt and get on with my life?

Sincerely,
Lost and Never Found

Dear Lost and Never Found,

The first thing you have to do is remind yourself that accidents happen. Heirlooms can be wonderful ways to connect generations, but they can also be a burden when people end up with things they're so stressed out about losing that they never use them.

The second thing you should do is explain to your mother what happened, and brace for what might be a less than ideal reaction. It sounds like the worry over telling her is eating you up, and you should just get it over with.

The third thing you should do is try social media. If you have a picture of the pendant, post it on social media specifically engaging with people who were at the event with you. Maybe someone picked it up without realizing the significance of it.

Maybe you and your mother could go out together and look for something that could be the new family heirloom. Every heirloom has to begin somewhere.

As for your great-great-great-grandmother, I hope she would understand. If nothing else, maybe she'll curse the person who took the pendant instead of cursing you.

Ask and I'll Answer,
Elodie

Early the next morning, I held my breath as I slowly pulled the blanket off of me and carefully put my foot on the floor. My mother stayed over to help me keep an eye on Aunt Erma. She was curled up and sleeping on the purple chair next to me. I begged her to sleep on the sofa, and I would sleep in the chair, but she refused. I figured she would sleep more soundly on the sofa, and I would have a better chance of sneaking out in the morning to go to the tree.

I crept over to the window. Mitzy stirred in Aunt Erma's room. Don't ruin this for me dog, I thought. As though she could hear me, she settled back in.

I pulled back the edge of the curtain. The snow had stopped, and there was just the faintest light in the sky. Good. I should have time to find the tree and get back before everyone woke up.

I was tiptoeing to the door when the phone rang. My mother leapt out of the chair.

"What's wrong?" she asked. Her eyes were wild with panic.

"It's the phone. I've got it," I said. The whole apartment was awake now. I cursed whoever was calling as I went over to answered it.

Flora was on the other end of the line. "Violet called. She wants you and Lena and I to go check out Lily Ridge," she said. Lily Ridge was another nearby town. "It looks like the IMPs have struck again."

"Already?" I groaned. This was a lot to take before I had my coffee.

"Can you be ready in five minutes?" she asked.

"Do you guys really need me?" I asked. I was still hoping to go find the magic tree.

"Violet thinks we might need your magic, and she doesn't think they realize how bad Erma is. Mr. Barnes will help your mother at the pie shop," she said. "Bring some of the spices. So see you in five."

I explained the situation to my mother as I threw on some jeans, a hooded sweatshirt, and my jacket. Downstairs in the kitchen, I opened the latch on the sparkly wooden box with the swirly designs where Aunt Erma kept her spices, and I grabbed a few bottles. When I got outside, Flora was already warming up her SUV. I had been surprised when I first found out Flora drove such a big vehicle.

"Books are heavy and take up a lot of space and sometimes I have to transport a lot of them," she explained. "And I wouldn't be able to do that if I drove a teensy little car like yours."

Lena came flying out of the front of the hardware store. She had just thrown boots and a coat over her red flannel pajamas. She skidded to a stop by the SUV before jumping in. "What is with these people?" she asked breathlessly. "Can't they take a few days off so we can enjoy the holiday season?"

"How could they not know how bad Aunt Erma is?" I asked. "They did this to her."

"They probably think the effects were just temporary. If they figure out that she's as bad as she is, they might try something bigger," Flora explained.

I thought about the tree and how it might fix everything. I desperately wanted to tell Flora and Lena about it, so they could help me, but I had made a promise to Aunt Erma. I knew she wouldn't understand if I broke her trust. Even in a dire situation like this.

I sighed and leaned back in the seat. Warm air was blowing out of the vents, and my eyelids felt heavy. Lena and Flora were talking strategy. I shook my head a little to wake up.

Apparently, the security cameras showed the residents of Lily Ridge gathering for a large cookie baking day.

"That doesn't sound any stranger than having a snowman building contest," I said.

"It is when it happens at four am," Lena said.

"Good point."

"Their magic could be stronger too, since they took that carving from Mr. Barnes's studio," Lena warned.

"Violet is worried that they've made more progress with their altered spices, and they want to do a widespread test of the effects, so they're doing it with cookies," Flora said.

We had a basic plan in place by the time Flora was pulling into a parking lot near the local grocery store. I was going to begin sprinkling Aunt Erma's original spices in the cookie dough. The magic in our spices was supposed to counteract the magic in the altered spices. Flora and Lena were supposed to start bagging the cookies that they'd already baked so we could get rid of them.

It was pretty easy to track down where everyone was. We just followed the smell of the cookies. After all the drama with Alice last month, cookies still made me shudder, but they sure did smell good.

I clutched the bottles of spices tightly in my hands as we walked towards the door of the bakery. It was a white stucco building. A large dark blue sign hung over the door. The words "Eastside Bakery" were painted in bold white letters. The door was propped open, but when we stepped inside, it was warm even on this frigid morning.

This scene was different than the chaos at the church where they were knitting the mitten. This time all of the people were focused and intense. They were working quickly and efficiently. That can't be good. They're definitely improving their spells.

We got to work. Flora fluffed up a couple of garbage bags, and she and Lena grabbed cookie sheets and dumped them into their bags. I was a little jealous that they had the fun job. After Alice, I felt like it would be satisfying to dump a bunch of cookies into the garbage.

I went to the giant mixer on the side of the kitchen that was mixing up a large batch of light brown dough. I sprinkled a healthy amount of Aunt Erma's spice number five in it. I carefully approached a man wearing a chef's hat who was rolling out a large sheet of dough. There were two men and a woman next to him. They were wearing their pajamas and cutting out shapes with cookie cutters. They all gazed at their work intently, pressing their cookie cutters down in quick systematic movements. I slowly reached in front of them to sprinkle spice on the dough they were working with.

"You're not supposed to be here," the man rolling the dough glared at me sharply. He had curly reddish-brown hair and a goatee. He was probably a lovely person when he wasn't under a spell. I glanced at Lena. Was this a normal part of the spell? Lena's pinched eyebrows clued me in that it wasn't.

"This must be a new addition to the spell," she said, just as a giant wad of cookie dough hit me in the face. The cookie dough was flying at me fast and furious from every direction. So far Lena and Flora were going undetected. Voices kept yelling, "You're not supposed to be here." I threw another dash of the spice on the cutouts on the table and dodged the flying dough when I could. I added a little spice to the open bag of flour for good measure and then ran out the front door. And straight into Josh.

"Your mother mentioned you were here," he said. "I came because we still need to talk."

"This isn't a great time," I said, wiping a giant glob of cookie dough out of my hair. I glanced behind me. No one had followed me out.

He surveyed me as though realizing for the first time that something was off. "What's going on here?"

"Nothing, just a food fight," I said with a nervous chuckle, and I led him away from the scene in case anyone decided to check to make sure I was gone. We went around the corner, and I saw he had parked his dark blue truck next to Flora's yellow SUV. Once we were a safe distance away, I said, "So you wanted to talk. Let's talk."

"I can't have a serious conversation with you when you're covered in...what are you covered in?" he asked.

"Cookie dough." I felt a blob slide down my back and shifted uncomfortably. "It's part of this small-town Christmas scavenger hunt." I waved it off as though any further explanation would bore him. "How's the job going?"

"Good," he said. "They've changed the fixtures in the bathrooms six times, but hopefully this time they'll stick."

Lena and Flora rounded the corner, each dragging four bags of cookies.

"Start the car," Lena yelled. I didn't have the keys for the SUV, but I ran to help them. Josh was right beside me and grabbed three of the bags. There was a mob of people chasing us. They wouldn't all fit in Flora's car, so we threw some in the back of Josh's truck. Somehow in the chaos, Lena ended up in Josh's truck, and Flora and I were in the SUV. We all sped off.

I hoped Lena would be able to explain this all to Josh. I didn't envy her being in that position, but she was a smooth talker.

During the drive, I apologized several times to Flora for getting cookie dough all over her car seat. She assured me she could clean it off in no time. When we got back to Hocus Hills we pulled the cars around behind the pie shop so we could dispose of the bags of cookies in the dumpster. Aunt Erma must have heard the commotion because she stuck her head out.

"Hi Aunt Erma," I said, hoping beyond hope that she would answer me normally.

"Sometimes I steal rolls of toilet paper from restaurants," she said.

"Oh, Aunt Erma," I laughed. Lena and Flora joined in glancing at Josh. We threw the bags in the dumpster. Aunt Erma sized Josh up.

"You don't belong in this world. You're not safe here," she said. He raised his eyebrows and looked at me.

Flora quickly ushered Aunt Erma back inside. I grabbed Josh by the corner of his sweatshirt and led him back towards his truck.

"She's been really stressed out," I said. "I don't think she's sleeping very well." He politely accepted this explanation. "Just a sec," I said, and I jogged over to Lena. She was just about to go inside too.

"Hey, I have something I have to go take care of," I said in a low voice, eyeing Josh meaningfully.

"Say no more." She nodded knowingly. "We have things under control here." She disappeared inside.

I went back over to Josh. "It seems like you're busy. Maybe we can talk another time," he said.

"Yeah, we'll talk soon," I said. I was about to give him a hug when I realized I was still covered in cookie dough. So I just waved instead. I took this opportunity to run to my car. I was going to find the magic tree.

I shook off as much cookie dough as I could. A lot of it had dried and fell off in sugary crumbs. I turned my coat inside out so I wouldn't get my car too dirty. A little dough still smeared across the seat as I slid in. I was trying to keep a low profile as I drove through town, so I crouched down in the seat as though that would keep people from recognizing me. The loud mufflerless red car certainly wouldn't tip them off.

I merged onto the highway and tried to visualize which exit Aunt Erma had taken. That one looks familiar. I pulled off and drove until I found a dirt road. Had there been a rock on the corner last time? I didn't remember a rock.

I turned around and tried a different road and then a different one, but I couldn't find the spot. I even got out of the car a couple times to wander through the woods, but I was afraid to wander too far away from the car because the last thing I needed was to get lost in the woods. I never watched those survival shows closely enough, and I didn't know how to do things like start a fire or find clean water and food. Lena told me once that there's a spell to start fires, but Aunt Erma refused to teach it to me. Probably because of the one, OK two times, I almost burned down the pie shop. These thing could happen to anyone.

I wearily drove back to the pie shop, my stomach swirling with the anxiety of failure.

Chapter 11

Dear Elodie,

Three years ago, I lost my husband in a car accident. I miss him every day, and it's a thousand times worse at the holidays. I have a friend who regularly texts me pictures of her and her husband doing different things, especially around the holidays. Her and her husband with Santa, her and her husband on a sleigh ride, her and her husband skiing. Every picture she sends crushes my spirit a little more, and I get stuck dwelling on how I can't do those things with my husband.

I don't think she knows what her pictures are doing to me, but I don't know how to stop her from sending them to me without seeming rude and bitter.

For the past two years, every time we're together, she tells me about the latest guy she's met that she wants to set me up with. I try to tell her I'm not ready, but she just brushes it off, saying I don't know what's good for me.

We've been friends for a long time. She was really there for me after my husband died. I still miss my husband, and I'm not ready to meet someone new yet.

How do I handle this situation? Do I just need to toughen up?

Sincerely,
Single and not ready to mingle

Dear Single and not ready to mingle,

It sounds like your friend's heart might be in the right place, but her actions definitely leave a little to be desired. You said she's a good friend. She probably sees your unhappiness and is trying to fix it. That is certainly easier said than done. Try to sit down with your friend, and have a frank conversation about how her actions are affecting you. Tell her that you're very happy for her, but you're still struggling, and her pictures and constant matchmaking attempts aren't helping. You will find someone if and when you're ready to.

You asked if you need to toughen up. The answer is no. Your grief isn't on anyone else's schedule. However, if you're feeling like the weight of this all is too heavy, you should really seek counseling. A counselor might help you deal with your grief, especially during the holidays. There are also a lot of support groups out there with people who are feeling the same way you are.

Ask and I'll Answer,
Elodie

Mr. Barnes was the first of the Morning Pie Crew through the door the next day. The morning rush had come and gone, people rushing in to pick up their pies for whatever holiday event they had going on that day. I had just finished wiping off the front tables.

Aunt Erma was still spilling all of her secrets, but at least her frantic rearranging had stopped. We had been telling people that she had the flu so word wouldn't get out that she was under a bad spell. I think people were buying it too. Three people had brought in soup for her and another four had brought in their "special elixirs."

We had managed to focus Aunt Erma on the great task of organizing photos for photo albums. She had boxes and boxes of pictures in her closet. A couple weeks ago she had gone digging in her closet for a stuffed monkey I had given her when I was five, and she knocked over a tall stack of boxes. Pictures had spilled out onto the floor, and Aunt Erma and I shoved them back into the boxes haphazardly and stacked them back up. When I told her that she could scan them all so they'd be available digitally, she looked at me like I'd grown a second head.

She seemed content with sorting the photos by date, so we left her upstairs with her very diligent guard dog, Mitzy. My mother and I worked in the pie shop.

Mr. Barnes didn't greet me with his usual wide smile, but he gave me a hug and squeezed me tighter than normal. "Are you busy?" he asked, "You can keep working. I'll just sit here with the paper."

"I'm never too busy for you," I said carrying two coffees out to the table where he was sitting out front.

He smiled, but I could see his eyes were a little watery through his glasses.

"What's on your mind today?" I asked, setting the steaming mug in front of him.

"It's just this time of year," he said. "I love it and hate it at the same time. It makes me miss my wife terribly."

A tear fell down his cheek, and I swallowed hard trying to keep any from coming to me. I knew he had a wife. Flora had told me once. I knew she died ten years ago, but I didn't know much more than that. Mr. Barnes didn't talk about her often. I think it was too painful. I didn't ask any questions because I didn't want to pry and upset him. Today he was in the mood to talk though.

"She really loved Christmas," he said staring into his coffee. "I still have all the boxes of decorations that she used to put all over our house, but I can't use them. I've tried taking them out of the storage room before, but every time I do, I just remember that she's not here to put them up, and I end up shoving them back in the room until the next year when I go through the same routine."

"The holidays can be tough," I said, thinking of my dad. I always thought about him this time of year. About what the holidays would be like if he was still here. They had always felt so empty after he died. Probably because that marked our separation with Aunt Erma too. With the four of us, the house was always bustling and happy, but when it was just the two of us, me and my mother, it felt empty and sad. My mother had tried to make up for it. She really did, but I knew she was sad too. She would invite people to celebrate with us. The last few years, Josh would sometimes join us. His family lived in Texas, and he couldn't always get home for the holidays. So, on those holidays, we adopted him.

"I just keep wondering why her," he said. "I know it's selfish, but why couldn't it have been me? Why couldn't I have died instead. But there must be a reason I'm still here, right?"

"Yes," I said. "I'm sure your wife was a lovely person, but you're a lovely person too. You were lucky to have found the love of your life."

"But how is it lucky when I just have to endure the pain of losing her?" he asked.

Well that was a tough question. I certainly didn't have a good answer. "Maybe it's not that you're supposed to feel the pain, maybe it's her mission on this earth was done, but yours isn't. When my dad died, Aunt Erma told me he was still here in some way. That I could still talk to him."

"I know, I feel like my wife is still close too. I talk to her a lot. She would have loved you," he said. "With magic we're even closer to the other side than most people are. Do you feel that more now?"

"Maybe. Sometimes. A little," I said.

"You should come to my yoga class this afternoon," he said. "We go deep into meditation. That's when I feel closest to my wife. Maybe you would feel closer to your dad then."

"I'll try that," I said. "I like the idea of being closer to him. I wonder if I could get my mother to come."

"I've worked hard trying to get her to come to my classes. So far, she's refused. Sometimes with fairly colorful language. She seems like someone who could really use some yoga in her life," he said.

"I do not disagree with that statement," I said with a chuckle. I looked at him for a minute. He was staring at a spot on the table. His lip was quivering. "I'm sorry about your wife."

He met my gaze. His eyes were full of tears now. Mine were too.

"I'm sorry about your dad."

I hugged Mr. Barnes, and we both cried for a minute together. When he pulled away, he told me a joke about fish, and I told him a joke about doughnuts. We were laughing and on our second cup of coffee by the time the rest of the Morning Pie Crew came.

Before he left, Mr. Barnes batted his eyelashes at me and asked if I could stop by the yoga studio sometime today and take a look at the heater.

I grabbed my tool bag and headed to the yoga studio during another lull in the action at the pie shop. My mother had everything under control, and Aunt Erma still seemed happy with her task of sorting photos.

When I stepped inside the studio, I wasn't greeted with the usual blast of warm air. Mr. Barnes was sitting in the corner watching television on his small flat-screen TV. He switched it off when I walked in.

"I'm so glad you could come," he said. "Lena tried to fix it, but she couldn't figure out what was wrong. For the last week it's been acting strangely. Sometimes it was running hot, sometimes it was running cold, and finally it just stopped running altogether. I've had to try to convince the classes the last couple days that this is a new kind of yoga. Lukewarm yoga instead of hot yoga. I don't think they're buying it."

"Hopefully I can get you back up and running," I said. The heater was by the ceiling, and Mr. Barnes went to the closet to pull out a step stool for me. I climbed up and unscrewed the corners, so I could lift the front panel off.

I got to work, and he made small talk. I usually like to work alone, so I can focus, but I didn't want to be rude and ask him to leave his own studio.

"How's your magical education going?" he asked.

"It's been a bit hit and miss." I stepped off the stool to grab a pliers. "I seem to only get half the spells right. Everyone says I'm powerful, but apparently you can't always make up for in power what you lack in knowledge."

"That's very true." Mr. Barnes had pulled a rag out of the closet and was dusting the shelves around the studio now.

"Aunt Erma's a patient teacher though."

"She's a powerful woman too," he said. "Does she ever talk about where her power comes from?"

I hit the test button on the heater and hot air blew into my face. "I think I got you back up and running," I said. I ignored his question and hoped he wouldn't ask it again. Then I stepped down to get away from the hot air. I let it run for a minute, watching it closely for any signs that it might falter. I could feel

Mr. Barnes watching me out of the corner of my eye. Once I was satisfied that the heater was fixed, I turned it off, grabbed the cover, and screwed it back in.

"Do you think Aunt Erma expects me to stay in Hocus Hills?" I asked.

He looked a little taken aback. "I don't know if she expects anything from you, but I think she'd like you to stay." I nodded, my brow furrowed as I tightened the last screw.

He thanked me for my help as I headed out the door.

"Will I see you for class tonight?" he asked hopefully.

"I think so," I said noncommittally.

After the steamy studio, the gust of cold air hit me hard as I stepped outside. I jogged back to the pie shop and burst in through the back door.

My mother was standing inside next to the sink. She held the phone in one hand and her other hand was on her hip. I'd seen that stance before. It was never good. She hung up the phone and glared at me.

"Hey, Mom," I said cheerfully. "How's Aunt Erma doing?"

"I just talked to Nina, and she said you were offered a job at Top-Notch Construction," she said, accusingly.

"How did she even know that?" I set down my tool bag at the edge of the desk at the back.

"Her son-in-law is Buster's daughter's lawyer," she said, "People talk."

Wow, and I thought that was just in small towns. "Yes, he offered me a job," I said.

"Why didn't you tell me?" she asked.

"Because I don't know if I'm going to take it," I said. I picked up a pen from a jar on the desk and twirled it between my fingers.

"What do you mean? Of course, you're going to take it." She began furiously wiping down the counters.

"I want more time here, with all of this." I pointed my pen around the kitchen.

"You can come here and visit."

"You know, some people might consider a thirty-two-year-old to be old enough to make her own decisions."

"Some thirty-two-year-olds would make the right decisions," she was now scrubbing an imaginary spot on the counter so hard, I thought she might hurt herself.

I opened my mouth, about to say something completely rational and profound, but Mitzy began barking before I could speak. I ran upstairs, my mother close behind me. We burst through the door.

"Aunt Erma, what's wrong?" I asked breathlessly.

"She has to go outside," she pointed at Mitzy, not even glancing up from her pictures. My mother and I looked at each other for a minute. Our fight would have to be put on hold. I took Mitzy outside.

Later that afternoon, I was stepping inside the yoga studio for the meditation class. All my shivering muscles relaxed in the warmth. The heater must still be working. I looked over at Mr. Barnes, and he gave me a thumbs up. I began to shed all the layers I had put on over my leggings and tunic tank top. Only four of us had signed up for the class. The two women worked at the Mexican restaurant. I think the man had come into the pie shop once or twice. I recognized his wavy white hair and easy smile. The other three looked a lot calmer than I felt. Mr. Barnes had lit candles around the room. There was soothing guitar music playing softly.

"Everyone go ahead and grab your yoga mat and sit down," he said. Go ahead and be close to your neighbors. You can feed off each other's energies." I rolled out my yoga mat in the far corner.

I had been to some of Mr. Barnes's yoga classes before, but this time I felt an anxious fluttering in my stomach. When I came to the regular yoga classes, I accepted that I was going to make a fool of myself. I'd try to do the tree pose, then yell "Timber," and fall to the ground. Then I would spend most of the class dreaming about the part at the end when we'd get to lay on the floor.

The stakes were higher this time. This time I wanted to feel closer to my dad.

Mr. Barnes began to walk us through some gentle stretches and breathing exercises. I really wished I hadn't had three cups of coffee before coming here. I could feel my feet twitching even after he had told us to lay down on our backs perfectly still on our mats.

"Just stop all movement," I heard his voice closer to me. I curled my toes, scolding them for their unruly behavior. "Deep breath in and begin to feel all your tension slide out of your body."

I took the breath in and slowly let it out. Hey, it was working. I felt some of the tension and energy in my muscles drift away. "Take another deep breath and focus on slowly inhaling until your lungs are full and gently release your exhale. Focus only on your breath. The room is warm. You are safe. In here there are no to do lists. In here there are no expectations. There is just you." His voice was smooth and low.

I tried to be in the moment and not to think about all the pies I had to bake or the apartment I had to find or the presents I had to buy. I really wanted this to work, so I tried **not** to think about how badly I wanted this to work. I felt myself sliding deeper down in my mind. Was I falling asleep? I listened to Mr. Barnes's voice, but I wasn't really paying attention anymore. I was just thinking about my dad.

98

"Dad, where are you?" I thought.

Suddenly I saw the highway in front of me. I was zooming along. Am I meditating right? I wondered as I exited and took a turn down a dirt road. Wait, this was familiar. I was heading towards the magic tree.

"Well this was unexpected," I heard a voice that was definitely not my father's. My eyes were still closed, but a face popped up in my mind. A woman's face. She looked vaguely familiar, but I couldn't quite put my finger on it.

"Who are you?" I asked.

She scoffed, "Like you don't know." She rolled her eyes and at once I knew who she reminded me of.

"You're Alice's sister," I said.

"That's right. The one and only Nellie," she struck a pose. Her voice had an edge to it. With her dark hair and sharp eyes, she really did look like an evil fairy from a fairy tale.

"I'm not here to see you, I said. I tried to pull myself out. I listened for Mr. Barnes's voice, but I couldn't hear it anymore. "Wake up," I told myself. "Please wake up. This is just a dream." But nothing. I was still there in front of Nellie. She looked amused.

"Are you done?" she asked.

"I don't want to talk to you," I said.

"Sorry, Cookie, you're on my turf now," she said. "This conversation is over when I say it is."

"What do you want?" I asked.

"You know Erma's secret," she said.

"That she loves pickles?" I asked. I was listening hard for Mr. Barnes's voice. I wanted to get out of this state. Whatever this state was before this conversation went any further.

"I may not have accomplished all the things that I wanted to in the mortal world, but I can still show the IMPs where to find

Erma's secret," Nellie said. She was fishing. She didn't even know what the secret was. I tried not to think about the tree.

"Show me!" she cried.

The map appeared in the air for a second. She looked smug, and I yelled and lunged at her.

"Susie! Susie!" someone was calling my name. They sounded panicked. It wasn't Nellie's voice.

Suddenly I realized I was laying on the ground. I cracked an eye open. Mr. Barnes was standing over me with fear in his eyes. I felt out of breath and confused. I looked around, and the class was all staring at me.

"What?" I asked, innocently.

"You were yelling, and you wouldn't wake up," he said. His voice was still higher pitched than normal, but he looked more relieved now that I was talking to him.

"I must have dozed off," I lied. "I think I was having a bad dream. Sorry everyone." The rest of the class exchanged raised eyebrows, and I sat up.

"I'm going to call your mother," Mr. Barnes said. He stood up to get the phone.

"That's not necessary. I have to go." I rolled up my mat and grabbed my pile of clothes. I was out the door before he could stop me.

Chapter 12

I ran straight to my car. I was shivering by the time I slid into the driver's seat because I was still just wearing my tank top and leggings. I threw on a sweatshirt and some sweatpants. I had to get to the tree first.

I started up my car and sped down the road. Heads turned. I shouldn't be drawing this much attention to myself. The roads were still a little slippery after yesterday's snow, so I slowed down a fraction. I wouldn't be able to save Aunt Erma if I got into a car accident.

I had a feeling I would have some explaining to do once I got back. No doubt Mr. Barnes had called my mother. I would have to worry about that later. For now I went back to the things I saw during my meditation. I easily found the right exit this time. I wondered if Nellie was able to tell the IMPs what she knew right away. Aunt Erma had some pretty serious protection spells around the tree, but I wasn't sure it would be enough to keep them away if they went right to it.

I shuddered a little at the thought of Nellie hanging out inside my mind. How could I be sure she wasn't still in there somewhere. I would have to ask Aunt Erma when I got back.

The sun was beginning to lower in the sky as I turned onto the dirt road. I pressed the gas pedal a little harder. I really wanted to get out of the woods before dark. I knew exactly where to pull over. I jumped out of the car and ran in the direction of the tree. It was almost as though it was calling me. It was hard to run through the deep snow. I had to lift my feet really high as my shoes were filling with snow.

Finally, there it was still decorated and beautiful. I let out a strangled sob of relief. I approached it slowly, as though it may attack me without Aunt Erma. The leaves just rustled in the wind. The snow inside my shoes was beginning to harden into ice.

"What do I need to make her better?" I mused aloud.

A branch near my face shook dangling leaves in my face. I carefully pulled a couple off and put them in my pocket. Then I heard a slight scratching noise and I noticed a corner of the bark had come up. I scraped off a small chunk with my car keys. "Thank you," I whispered to the tree.

I don't know if I heard it or if I felt it first, but suddenly I knew that I wasn't alone. The hair on the back of my neck stood up. A twig snapped nearby. I couldn't see anyone through the trees, but it was getting darker and hard to make out much of anything. I held my breath and listened. All I could hear was my heart pounding in my chest.

Could it be an animal? I tried to remember what to do if I saw a bear. One kind of bear you were supposed to run from and one you were supposed to play dead for. Which one was which? Were there even bears in these woods? I wished I'd watched more of the nature channel and less reality television.

I was crouched down ready to scream and run because those seemed like the best options, when I heard what sounded like a dinosaur bounding through the woods. Fight or flight, fight or flight, I debated. I decided to hide next to the tree trunk, even though it was far too skinny to cover my body. I hoped that the magic would protect me.

A dark brown creature streaked past me. What was that? A coyote? A lion? A dragon? I was almost delirious with fear. I crouched closer to the tree trunk, and I could feel the magic. It tingled up my arm and through my body, warming me from the inside out. I no longer thought my feet were going to freeze and snap off. I closed my eyes and wished for everything to be OK so I could get back to Aunt Erma.

I could hear crashing through the woods and then a man's voice yelled, "Aaah, run!"

My eyes snapped open. The voice sounded familiar, but I couldn't tell who it was, and I still couldn't see anyone between the trees. More crashing, and I shivered despite the magic.

The sound was coming towards me now. I pulled out my phone thinking that I should at least call my mother and tell her where to find my body if I didn't make it back. I didn't get a signal way out here. Why did I decide to go to the magic tree alone? So what if it was a huge secret?

I tried not to scream as the crashing got closer. I didn't know who was still out in the woods. Then I saw him. A large dark brown dog running towards me. I held very still. Maybe he wouldn't see me. The dog came bounding up and sat at my feet, tail wagging furiously. I cautiously checked him for a collar, but he wasn't wearing one. I looked behind him, but he seemed to be alone.

"Where's your family?" I asked, quietly. I spent too much time with Mitzy and now expected all dogs to understand me.

He leaned his head against my leg, and I scratched him behind his ears.

"Thanks for your help, but shoo. You should go home now," I said. I had to get out of these woods before it was pitch black.

I began to jog back towards the car with magical tree bits in my pocket and ice bits crunching in my shoes. Suddenly I was face down in the snow. Ouch. I must have tripped over a tree branch. When I sat up, I was looking into two big brown eyes. The dog was following me.

"Go home," I said again, a little more harshly, as I continued to the car a little slower now. He ignored me and stayed close.

103

When I got back to the car, I opened the door, and the dog leapt in before I could stop him. "Hey," I cried, but he didn't seem to mind my protests. He just wagged his tail. "Yeah, you're funny. Now come on." I tried all the dog tricks I had learned from my few weeks with Mitzy. Excited voice. Firm voice. Ignoring. But nothing worked. The dog remained firmly planted in the car. I tried to push him out, but it seemed like he weighed a thousand pounds. From the look on his face, he wasn't at all bothered by my frustration.

"Fine, I'll take you home later." I gave in. I had to get this stuff back to Aunt Erma. The dog wagged his tail and as soon as I closed the door sat in the driver's seat. He licked my cheek. "Not cool, dog," I said, wiping my face off with the sleeve of my jacket.

By the time we got back to Hocus Hills, the dog was curled up sleeping in the back seat. I decided to worry about the new creature later.

"What in the world?" my mother asked when she saw the unfamiliar dog. He followed me inside like he belonged there.

"Don't ask," I said flatly.

"Stop right there," my mother said. The dog sat down.

I turned toward her and tilted my head. "What?" I asked brightly.

"Mr. Barnes called here." Of course he did. Tattletale. "Would you care to explain to me what happened at the yoga studio?"

"I'll admit, it got pretty wild. There was stretching and music and even," I paused dramatically, "candles burning." My mother was not amused. I let out a frustrated sigh. "Nothing happened. I was tired. I fell asleep. Then I had to run some errands. I'm going to go take a quick nap now. I'll be back soon to help close up." The dog got up to happily follow me upstairs.

"We're not done talking about this," my mother called. "And where on earth did that dog come from?"

Mitzy ran to greet me when I walked through the door, but then stopped dead in her tracks when she saw I wasn't alone. She sized him up. He was easily twice her size. She ran around him, sniffed him and jumped on him. He laid down, his tail wagging, and watched her run around in excited circles.

Aunt Erma was still sitting at the table going through photos. She looked up when I approached her. "Tea?" she announced with a firm nod.

"Is that what I do with this?" I asked, pulling the slightly smooshed leaves and chunk of bark out of my pocket.

"I like tea," she said.

"I'm going to make some," I said. I hoped that she would direct me at some point if I was doing it wrong, so I explained every step of the way. "I'm boiling some water," I said. "Then I'm going to steep these leaves and this bark in the water."

She tilted her head at me. "When I was nine, I used to write love letters to the actor from that monkey movie."

"Ok," I said. "After it's steeped for a few minutes, I'm going to strain it and pour it into a mug."

She winked at me. "Right on, Sugar," she said.

The dogs had now pulled all the blankets and pillows off the sofa, and they were now gleefully rolling on them. I yelled at them to stop, but those same ears that could hear a treat bag open from a mile away, suddenly couldn't hear me.

"Would you like honey, or does that mess with the tree's magic?" I asked Aunt Erma.

"I like to lick the edge of the honey jar when it drips," she said. I really hoped this tea worked. I couldn't handle all these truths for too much longer. I made a mental note not to use the honey anymore.

I let the leaves and the bark steep while I made up a spell to break the spell on Aunt Erma. She had told me that intention was very important when casting a spell, so I made sure my intention was pure and hoped that would be enough. Plus, the tree seemed to love Aunt Erma, so maybe it would work with me to free her from this evil spell. I paused for a second. It had been just a few weeks since I'd learned about magic and how it was real — a fact I hadn't even considered since I was a child, but here we were. I was believing that a tree could have good or bad intentions. I shook my head a little. Life's funny sometimes.

Once I thought the tea had brewed long enough, I carefully poured it into a green and blue caterpillar mug and handed it to her.

"Please drink this," I said. She looked at it and then looked at me. I was afraid for a moment she wouldn't drink it. I breathed a sigh of relief as she took a small sip. She wrinkled her nose and set the mug down on the counter. Apparently magic tree tea didn't taste good. I added some honey, trying not to touch the sides of the jar. I handed the mug back to her. She took another sip and smiled. She finished the magic tea.

I held my breath and watched her carefully. I was hoping to see sparkles around her or hear some magic music or something, but nothing.

"Thank you," Aunt Erma sighed. "It's good to be back."

I threw myself at her and she dropped the tea cup. It shattered on the floor.

"Oops," I said. Mitzy made a running leap and was in Aunt Erma's arms as soon as I was out of them. "It worked! It worked!" I danced around. Our new dog friend joined me as I danced a victory lap around the living room.

My mother rushed in brandishing a rolling pin. "What's happening? What's wrong?"

"Aunt Erma's back," I said, presenting her with a flourish of my arm.

Aunt Erma smiled at my mother. "That was truly an awful spell," she said. My mother ran towards her.

"Careful," I warned as my mother got close to the sharp bits of ceramic. "Mitzy broke a teacup." I pointed to the ground, and Mitzy gave me a death stare.

I felt a huge wave of relief now that we had Aunt Erma back to her usual self. Now we just had to stop the IMPs, and we could really focus on Christmas.

Chapter 13

Word spread fast, and the Morning Pie Crew was in the front of the shop laughing and hugging Aunt Erma in no time.

Lena pulled out a bottle of champagne and six champagne flutes from her giant yellow purse.

"To family, friends, and broken curses," Aunt Erma said, clinking glasses with everyone. I served everyone slices of chocolate coconut cream pie.

"What's the name of your new friend?" Flora asked.

I was confused until she explained. "That dog you brought home. What's his name?" she asked.

"I don't know," I said. "I'm waiting for his family to claim him. They'll know what his name is."

"Dear," Aunt Erma chimed in. "He's yours. You're his. It's a special magic that brings together a person and an animal, and you two belong together. You should figure out what his name is." The dog wagged his tail at me.

"Sure," I told her though part of me was still hoping someone would show up to take him home.

"And you can't just assign him a name," Mr. Barnes said.

"You have to say different names and sounds until he reacts. That's how you figure out what he's supposed to be called," Lena explained. I looked around at all of them, expecting one of them to crack and tell me they were just kidding, but they all looked back at me with earnest gazes. Even my own mother.

"Right," I said slowly.

The minute everyone was distracted by how cute Mitzy and No Name were together, I pulled Aunt Erma into the kitchen and told her about Nellie appearing while I meditated and the person in the woods near the magic tree.

Her brow was wrinkled. "I should go put some extra protection spells on the tree just in case," she said.

"I'll go with you," I said.

"No, you need to stay here and keep everyone distracted so they don't notice that I'm gone," she grabbed her keys and was out the back door before I could protest.

"Where's Erma?" was, of course the first words out of Lena's mouth the second I came back from the kitchen.

"She just had to . . ." I wracked my brain for an excuse. "Run upstairs to the bathroom," I finished lamely. "Her last meal was not sitting so well." I patted my stomach and gave a sympathetic grimace.

They accepted my explanation without further questions.

Sorry, Aunt Erma, I thought.

Aunt Erma returned quickly. She was a little flushed as she rushed back into the room.

"How are you feeling?" Mr. Barnes asked.

"Fine," she said.

I rose my eyebrows and gave her a look that I hoped would say, "Are you sure about that?" I patted my stomach a little.

"Did you drink that ginger tea I brought you?" I asked.

"Oh yes, that was extremely helpful," she said smoothly. "I'm all better now." She took a sip of her champagne.

She's a skilled liar, I thought.

Henry came in. "I heard there's a celebration going on," he said.

Lena poured him some champagne, and the topic switched from Erma's newly broken spell to Flora's birthday dinner the next night. Her birthday had been shoved to the back burner with everything else that was happening, but now that Aunt Erma was back, they decided the show must go on.

"We can use that time to strategize a little more," Flora said. "We have to stop the IMPs so we can stop living in fear."

"Susie's friend Josh is going to be there," my mom reminded everyone.

I noticed Henry's eyebrows go up ever so slightly, but the rest of his face remained calm.

"We'll have to be discreet then," Flora said.

The next day was busy with preparations for Flora's birthday dinner and making pies for the shop. Customers buzzed with the excitement of the upcoming holidays. They were able to focus more on Christmas and less on the potential evil takeover of our town.

I have to admit, I would have been more excited for dinner if I weren't so nervous about Josh and Henry sitting in the same room. I could already feel the tension, and neither of them was in the room yet. Maybe it will be fine, I told myself. Right, and maybe Santa and his elves will come to dinner.

I had been dying to ask if Santa was real, but I was pretty sure I would never live down the ridiculing if he wasn't. Maybe I could try asking Flora sometime. She was least likely to laugh in my face.

My new dog friend was eager to help. I was in charge of the salad. The kitchen in the apartment was small, and as I walked from one side to the other, he tried to anticipate my every step so he could take it first. I don't know if he was trying to help or trying to kill me.

Flora's only request for the night was that everyone dress festively. Once the salad was made, I changed into a red tunic and green leggings and patted myself on the back for my Christmassy outfit.

My mother of course, was in a classy maroon skirt and white blouse. Aunt Erma wore a sparkly red jumpsuit with a large Santa pin, or as I mentally called it, "My Segue into the

110

Santa Conversation" pin. She had gold bells hanging from every button on her jumpsuit, and she topped the outfit off with her large antlers.

Lena and Mr. Barnes had come over earlier in the day to help decorate the front of the pie shop. We blew up balloons, hung streamers, and draped garlands of paper flowers around the pie display case. Lena had brought over a banner that she made that said, "Happy Birthday, Flora!", and Mr. Barnes had brought extra fairy lights to wrap around everywhere. The place looked even more magical than usual.

My mother, Aunt Erma, and I were putting the finishing touches on the room while we waited for everyone to arrive. Much to their delight, the dogs had been invited to join the fun tonight. Mitzy ran around sniffing every corner of the pie shop in search of stray crumbs, and no name set up camp in front of the food table. He laid there with his head between his paws looking pitifully at anyone who made eye contact with him as though he hadn't just eaten a giant bowl of dog food upstairs.

"While we wait for everyone, let's get this party started," Aunt Erma said, hitting play on the boom box. I had tried to get Aunt Erma to upgrade her music system a couple weeks ago, but I didn't get very far.

"You could go digital and make playlists of your favorite songs," I had mentioned to her.

"But I have my favorite songs on CDs," she replied.

"With digital music, you don't have to keep switching your CDs to hear all your favorite songs in a row."

"Why are you trying to take away my CDs?"

"This would be even better than CDs."

Blank stare. "Never mind."

"Holly Jolly Christmas," began playing and Aunt Erma and I danced between the tables. Mitzy jumped around our feet, her tail wagging excitedly. The other dog just watched us from

111

his spot sprawled on the ground. My mother suddenly got very busy rearranging crackers on a tray, but I caught her doing a little shimmy when the tempo really picked up.

Flora and Lena arrived together. Lena's sweater had a Christmas tree across the front complete with lights that lit up. Flora was dressed up head to toe as an elf. "I'm wearing the clothes of my ancestors," she said.

"Flora, your ancestors didn't dress up in green pointy hats and bell shoes," Aunt Erma said.

"Don't ruin my fun," she replied. She did a little jig and the bells on her shoes jingled.

Violet came in a dark green business suit. I had a feeling that was the most festive thing she owned. Mr. Barnes arrived with his bright red fedora and a matching vest over a bright green shirt and brown pants. He topped off the looks with a snowman bow tie.

Josh was close behind him. "I didn't have anything festive enough," he said. "So, Mr. Barnes lent me these." He took off his jacket, revealing glittery candy cane suspenders.

"Classy," Flora said, approvingly.

I greeted Josh cautiously. I was pretty sure he would be well behaved tonight, but the last thing I was ready to handle was a public proclamation of love. Lena and Flora seemed almost giddy and were watching Josh closely. I think they were enjoying the show.

Henry texted that he was going to be late. Some fiasco was happening at the nursing home. "Don't ask," he texted. It must be bad.

We poured drinks for everyone and sat down. I carefully seated myself between my mother and Lena. My mother hopped up so quickly, I'm surprised she didn't get whip lash.

"Josh, sit here. I'm going to take a spot closer to the kitchen, so I can keep an eye on the food," she said smoothly.

I wanted to glare at her, but it seemed too obvious. Josh sat down next to me. I pretended to be engrossed in a conversation Mr. Barnes and Flora were having about his ingrown toenail.

"Merry Flora's Birthday," Josh said, bumping his knee gently against mine.

"Yeah, you too," I said. I smiled tentatively at him. Maybe he wanted to talk to me because he wanted to tell me that he was wrong when he professed his love to me. It was as if some huge mistake was made, and he just wanted be friends again.

"Remember last year when the Butler family hired us to hang Christmas lights all over their house, including around the toilet in the bathroom?" he asked.

"That part wasn't so bad. I thought the inside of the closets was a bit excessive though," I said laughing. Soon we were talking like the old friends we were.

I almost didn't notice when Henry walked in. He was wearing a bright blue sweater with a giant snowflake on it.

"Henry," voices chorused bringing Josh and I out of our conversation. He looked tired but gave the room a giant smile. He came over and squeezed my shoulder. "Hey you," he said. Then turned to Josh. "Good to see you again. How are you enjoying our town?"

"I love it here," he said. "The people here are so nice. I really feel welcome."

"That's so great," Henry said, but there was something in his voice that made me think he might not be thrilled Josh was feeling so at home in Hocus Hills.

I glanced up and noticed that Flora, Lena, Violet, Mr. Barnes, and Aunt Erma were all openly watching the conversation. The only thing they were missing was popcorn. At least my mom wasn't gawking, I thought, until I looked over and saw her watching form the kitchen doorway. She was holding a potato masher and an empty bowl.

"Do you need any help in there, Mom?" I asked jumping out of my chair.

"Let me help too," Henry said. I noticed he shot a look back towards Josh as he followed me.

"Go ahead and take a seat, Mom," I said. I took the masher out of her hand. She hesitated but then went to sit down with Josh. I breathed a sigh of relief, and Henry snuck a quick kiss.

"Be careful," I warned. "That's violating the health code."

"I'll risk the fine," he said, kissing me again.

"How was your day?" I asked.

"It was Christmas cookie baking day," he said with low dread in his voice. "I had to go home and shower before coming here. I had flour in places I didn't know I could have flour."

"Oh no," I laughed.

"It wasn't as bad as your most recent cookie experiences though, so I really can't complain." He helped me drain the potatoes, so we could start mashing them.

"What cookie experiences?" Josh appeared in the doorway of the kitchen.

"I had a minor feud with a woman who owned a cookie shop in town," I said. "She's not here anymore though." I kept my eyes on the mashed potatoes, only glancing up once to see how he was taking my vague story. He just nodded.

"Could you put these on the table?" I asked holding out the giant bowl.

We all sat down at the crowded table. I sat next to Henry, but directly across from Josh. Flora was at the head of the table.

Flora clinked her wine class with her knife to get everyone's attention. The group quieted down, except for Lena who began composing her symphony by clinking all the glasses around her with her knife. She bobbed her head to the beat.

"It's going to be your job to take away her wine glass," Flora told Josh with a wink.

"Oh no, I would never touch another person's wine glass," he said holding his hands up.

Lena wrapped up her song and gave us all a serene smile. We turned our attention to Flora.

Flora gave a heartfelt toast about how lucky she was to be surrounded by such wonderful friends and family. I glanced around the table. Through my tears I could see I wasn't the only one getting misty eyed. Henry was using his napkin to wipe away a tear on his cheek, and Mr. Barnes had removed his glasses. Aunt Erma and Lena were both sniffing. Violet was blinking hard. My mother was staring intensely at a spot on the ceiling. Even Josh's brow was wrinkled with emotion. When she was done, we all cheered with tears in our eyes.

Dinner was delicious. The chatter was so loud I could hardly hear the Christmas music in the background.

After everyone helped clear the table, the strategy sessions began. The groups began to rotate so that at least one person was always watching Josh. My mother seemed more than happy to keep him in a magic free zone. She kept trying to pull me into their conversations. I think she was still hoping that I would leave this magic life and return home to marry Josh. I wouldn't be surprised if she began calling him "son" after one more glass of red wine.

"The ice show is tomorrow," Violet told me, Henry, Flora, and Aunt Erma while Mr. Barnes regaled Josh and my mother with tales of his last yoga retreat. "They might try something there. It's a big town event. After the snowman building competition, the last thing we need is to have a bunch of ice skaters attacking the crowd." Lena shuddered at the thought.

We kept rotating into different groups as we made a plan so Josh wouldn't get suspicious. It was like a giant game of telephone, and the more wine that was consumed, the more jumbled the plan got. In the end I think Henry and I had volunteered to stake out the ice show and keep an eye out for any IMP activity. Violet recruited Lena and Aunt Erma to help her watch the security camera feeds from around town, and Flora and Mr. Barnes would drive around town looking for anything strange that the security cameras might miss. I hoped one of us would remember the plan.

"Goodnight everyone," I said a little too loudly as they all shuffled out the door sometime after midnight.

Josh lingered for a minute, but so did Henry. After an awkward moment, Josh said a quick goodbye and left.

"I can't wait to go to the ice show with you," Henry said once we were alone. Well, kind of alone. Aunt Erma was in the other kitchen and there were two dogs sitting in the middle of the room, tails thumping as they wagged. Their unblinking eyes stayed fixed on us.

"This would be so much more romantic if we weren't on the lookout for psycho villains," I said.

"We can make it romantic." He gently brushed the hair out of my eyes and put his hand behind my neck, pulling me in for a kiss.

I heard what sounded like a sneeze from the next room. Or was it laughter? I really had to get my own place, so my new love life wasn't critiqued from the next room. The second Henry was gone, Aunt Erma came out of the kitchen. It was almost as though she had been listening to us.

"What do you think? Should we finish cleaning up in the morning?" she asked.

"Definitely," I agreed.

I took the dogs outside, and Aunt Erma went up to get ready for bed. When we got upstairs, Aunt Erma was in her room reading. Instead of joining her like she usually would, Mitzy stayed in the living room, gazing adoringly at her new friend. The dark brown dog stared at me as I laid down on the sofa.

"What's your name, buddy?" I asked. I decided to try Henry's method and began to list names to see if the dog would react. Maybe if I could at least figure the sound out, I could guess his name.

I began to sing the alphabet song. The dog laid down, but kept staring at me. His tail began to wag when I got to G but then I heard a rumbling noise and realized he was just passing gas. Mitzy stood and took a few steps back, but her loving gaze never faltered.

"Fluffy?" I tried. He closed an eye. "Rover?" He closed the other. I went through Larry, Bob, Gigi, Puppy, Bubba — all without a reaction. I kept going, I began just naming object in the room. "Phone, Table, Sofa, Rug." All turned out not to be his name. I moved on to food. "Pizza, Pie, Raisin, Margarita, Lemon, Apple, Burrito." No reaction. "Coffee. Cake. Doughnut." At the last one, he opened his eyes. "Doughnut," I tried again. He didn't move, but he watched me.

"It's probably something that starts with a D," Aunt Erma called from the other room.

"Dooey, Darryl, Diego, Drake, Dakota, Daniel," I tried. Mitzy had settled into a spot on the back of the sofa and was now snoring loudly.

While I kept listing D names, I pulled one of Mitzy's tennis balls out from under the sofa. "Do you want to play, Donald?" I asked. I gently bounced the ball towards him. It hit him in the side, but he didn't even move. Mitzy heard her second favorite toy being used and flew off the back of the sofa to retrieve it.

117

"You have to read your doggie handbook because that's what you're supposed to do," I pointed at Mitzy. He seemed unconcerned.

I looked up D names on the internet and read through the list. By the time I was nearing the end, both dogs were sound asleep. When I said, "Duncan," that all changed. The big dog was on his feet and hurdled towards me, his tail wagging furiously. He got three licks on my face before I was able to sit up and push him away.

Aunt Erma came out of her room looking a little sleepy. "You figured it out?" she asked.

"Yes, I'd like to introduce you to Duncan," I said. Duncan sat at her feet and proudly wagged his tail.

"Hello, Duncan. Nice to officially meet you." She shook his paw in her hand. "That's strange," Aunt Erma said looking over at the phone table. She hadn't yet fully transitioned to cell phones. She still had a rotary dial phone on a table next to an answering machine. The light was blinking on the machine. "I thought I checked this when I first came upstairs. I didn't hear it ring, did you?" I shook my head. She hit the play button.

I heard an unfamiliar voice say, "Erma, when are you coming back? We miss you." Aunt Erma went pale and hit the stop button so quickly she almost knocked the machine off the table.

"Who was that?" I asked.

"No one," she said so quickly I'm surprised she even heard my question. Aunt Erma said goodnight and disappeared into her bedroom.

That was strange.

Chapter 14

Dear Elodie,

The other day I used my boyfriend's phone to make a call because mine was dead. While I was on it, a text came in from a woman he works with. Curiosity got the best of me, and I clicked on the message. I saw that they'd been texting each other for months at all hours, day and night. There's nothing particularly juicy in the messages, just a lot of friendly (and what could be interpreted as flirtatious) banter. This makes me very uncomfortable, but I don't know what to do now.

Do I confront my boyfriend? If I do, I have to admit that I was snooping through his phone. If I don't confront him, I think it will eat away at our relationship. Please help me figure out how to fix this.

Sincerely,
Sorry I Snooped

Dear Sorry I Snooped,

You have to talk to your boyfriend about it. Don't make it a confrontation, make it a conversation. You'll have to admit that you snooped, and you can apologize for violating his privacy. But tell him that now that it's out there, you need to talk about it. Most likely, he'll deny that anything inappropriate is going on, and it's up to you to decide if you believe him or not. It's possible for people to have emotional affairs without having a physical one. *You two have to talk about whether or not you're getting what you want out of your relationship with each other. Problems in a relationship can be fixed as long as both parties in the relationship are open to fixing them.*

> *Ask and I'll Answer,*
> *Elodie*

The next morning, Aunt Erma had left the apartment before I woke up. By the time I got down to the kitchen downstairs, my mother was there, and I couldn't ask about the voicemail.

We had a lot of special holiday orders people were picking up today. Three different people had ordered rum raisin pies. Why anyone would special order that was beyond me. Raisins made me want to gag, so I quickly offered to make the peanut butter silk. My mother made the rum raisin, and Aunt Erma worked on the berry pies. There were a couple of special orders for boysenberry pie and twenty-seven orders for her famous blueberry pie.

The second we unlocked the door, we had customers. The usual midmorning lull never came. People came in to pick up their orders, eat a slice of pie with out of town family and friends, and apologetically place last minute special orders.

I didn't have any time to worry about the strange voicemail from last night. I was serving customers out front while my mom and Aunt Erma kept baking and washing dishes in the back.

Lena called to ask if we should meet at the pie shop or the hardware store.

I was silent on the other end of the phone.

"You forgot about our appointment, didn't you?" she asked.

"No," I said slowly while wracking my brain.

"I'm taking you apartment hunting," she said. Lena not only ran the hardware store, she was also a realtor.

"Right!" Our conversation from the night before came back to me now. "I'll meet you at your place in a few minutes."

I went into the kitchen. "Can you guys spare me for an hour?"

My mother said, "No," just as Aunt Erma said, "Yes."

"Great, I'll hurry back," I said. I grabbed my coat and rushed out the back door before the conversation could go any further.

I was still feeling a little conflicted about staying in Hocus Hills. Sometimes I missed the bustle of the city, and then there was the wonderful job offer to consider. Then there was Josh. I hadn't decided if he was in the plus column or the negative column on the list of reasons to move back to the city.

I decided that it couldn't hurt to see what my apartment options were. I had been sleeping on Aunt Erma's sofa for too long, and now that I apparently had a dog, the apartment was getting a little crowded. Plus, I'd had one too many dates that included Aunt Erma and Mitzy. Henry had his own house, but his large dog, Willy, wasn't sure that he liked me as much as Henry did. He would sit in the middle of the living room and watch me through narrowed eyes. That's a little unsettling when you're trying to make out a little on the sofa.

Then of course it was impossible to have any privacy at a restaurant in a town like Hocus Hills. Henry was well liked, and it was not uncommon for people to stop by our table to chat for five to fifty minutes. I liked the small town charm, and the fact that people adored Henry, but it was awfully difficult to get into the romantic mood when Bill Carter stopped by to tell us a graphic twenty minute story about his latest bout of food poisoning. I ended up telling the waitress, "Thanks, but I'm not hungry anymore," when she brought out my bowl of vegetarian chili.

There were a few customers in the store when I got there. Lena was helping a woman pick out a light switch. She came over to me when she was done.

"It looks like you're keeping busy," I said.

"All those little projects that pile up over the course of the year are suddenly getting done because the in-laws are coming to stay for a week, and they expect to have a working door knob on the bathroom," she said.

"I don't want to take you away from your store," I said.

"Don't worry. Denny's got it covered," she said. Denny was the nineteen-year-old that Lena had hired for the holidays. He was quiet and a little sullen, but his lanky appearance and awkward manner reminded me a little too much of Stan, the former delivery man who was working with the IMPs to take over our town. Because of the resemblance, I usually avoided the hardware store if I knew Denny was working. That was really a tragedy because I loved going to the hardware store.

The second we stepped outside, Lena went into full real estate agent mode. "Don't you just love this time of year?" she asked. "There are no bad views in this town when it's all decorated for the holidays. And everywhere that I'm going to show you is conveniently located near the pie shop and near all the necessities, like the grocery store and the restaurants."

"Lena," I said, laughing. "If you're showing me any apartment in town, I'll be conveniently located near all the necessities."

"Well," she sniffed indignantly. "I think you'll like the ones I picked out anyway."

"I'm sure I will," I said. "You don't have to sell me on the town."

"I've heard rumors you're still running a little hot and cold on our town," she said. "There's a lot of pressure for me to perform. You should have heard the lecture Flora and Mr. Barnes gave me on the importance of finding you a place that you would love. Even Henry called and told me to pull out all the stops. When I was in the grocery store, Holly wouldn't check me out unless I promised to show you the place over on Sparkle Street," she said all this without hardly taking a breath. "Apparently Sparkle Street is an acceptable distance from Holly so that you guys can hang out and still walk home from each other's places after a few glasses of wine without getting lost."

"I see," I said. No wonder Lena was laying it on thick. There was an awful lot of pressure associated with where I lived.

"Erma will probably stop speaking to me once she hears I've taken you out apartment hunting. She doesn't think you should move until after we stop the IMPs." She threw up her arms. "I just can't win sometimes."

"I'm sorry everyone's been giving you such a hard time," I said. I put my arms around her and gave her a big hug.

"It's alright. I can take it," she said with a sniff. "Let's not worry about any of them now though," she switched back to her realtor voice. "Let's focus on you and what you want."

Lena was right, the first apartment did have wonderful views. It was on the second floor and looked down on the town square. The apartment itself had dingy gray walls and was about the size of a broom closet, but it did have a nice view. Lena kept pointing to the dusty window.

"It's nice," I said, trying to force a smile. We were a little too close to Alice's old cookie shop for my taste. Even though she was gone, her bad vibes still haunted me. I was hoping with enough yoga I could get past my dislike of this corner of the town square. But it wasn't going to happen overnight, so we left that first apartment pretty quickly.

123

"I thought it might be a little too close to that spot," Lena said, watching me out of the corner of her eye.

I just shrugged and smiled.

We didn't stay long at the second apartment either. It was a one bedroom on the first floor. Phyllis, the current tenant, was there. She had lived in the apartment for the last thirty years, but now she was moving into the nursing home. Her light blue sweater matched her eyes, and she kept her white hair in a low bun. When she smiled, the number of wrinkles on her face doubled. She was there because she wanted to give me a heads up about a few "quirks." Like apparently the hot water went out every couple of weeks. "There's something really refreshing about taking a cold shower," Phyllis said to my look of disbelief. "And you're just going to love Luther," she said.

"Who's Luther?"

"He lives upstairs, and he is the most talented tap dancer I've ever seen. He works the late shift at the diner, so he usually starts practicing around midnight. He's really dedicated too. He practices for two or three hours. And it's so funny, his dog will howl the entire time he's dancing. I think he's singing along. I just love listening to them," she said. I had backed out the door before she was even finished talking.

"Thanks, Phyllis. Good luck with the move," Lena said. "So, we'll put that on the maybe list?" Lena asked with a sly smile as we walked down the street.

The third apartment was the one on Sparkle Street. I simultaneously loved and hated then name. On the one hand, it was adorable. On the other hand, I was embarrassed at the thought of giving directions. "Turn left on Sparkle Street. It's the third shimmering building on your right."

The building was actually brick. It was right next to the grocery store, Basil's Market, where Holly and her mom Luanne worked. The apartment was on the third floor. It was a studio in the corner of the building so two of the walls had fairly large windows. The kitchen was tiny, but outside of the pie shop, I didn't really do a lot of cooking anyway. The appliances were a mint green as though straight out of the sixties. I liked the retro vibe. It had creaky dark wood floors, and the bathroom was almost as big as the rest of the apartment with a giant walk-in shower.

"Have you seen this shower?" I asked Lena as I stood in the middle of it and marveled at the two shower heads. The bathroom had white and black checkered tiles, which could be a lot to process in the morning, but I liked it.

"I was saving the best for last," she said. "This one is available right away, and the landlord is willing to do a month-to-month lease so you don't even have to commit for a whole year."

There was really no reason for me not to do it. "This is the place," I said with a decisive nod. Soon Henry and I could have a little alone time. I smiled at the thought.

"What are you thinking about?" Lena asked when she noticed my smile.

"Nothing," I said, blushing.

"Uh huh," she said knowingly.

When I got back to the pie shop, I jumped right in serving customers so I didn't have to answer any questions about where I'd been. On the flip side, I didn't have a chance to ask Aunt Erma about the voicemail. She and I were never alone, and she conveniently left to run an errand just as we were getting ready to close. My mom said she could clean up and sent me upstairs to get ready to go to the ice show.

The dogs were excited to see me. I took them outside and when we got back Mitzy busied herself trying to squeak her stuffed pig to death. Duncan grabbed the pig from her and rested his head on it. Having another dog in the apartment really could come in handy.

I wandered around for a few minutes. Something just seemed off with Aunt Erma. What if she was still under a spell? I didn't know what I was looking for. I picked up pieces of paper and looked behind picture frames. Duncan stood up and walked over to the table where Aunt Erma still had piles of pictures sitting out. She put her sorting project on hold once the spell was broken.

"Is there something here?" I asked, looking down at the pictures. Her tail wagged harder. Mitzy began to growl behind Duncan. Duncan turned and gave her one bark, and Mitzy stopped, but kept glaring at us. Duncan skillfully ignored Mitzy's gaze.

I picked up one pile. It was mostly pictures of the Morning Pie Crew dressed up in costumes. I assumed it was for Halloween, but with this crowd I couldn't be sure. The next stack was mostly pictures of Mitzy as a puppy.

"Mitzy, you were so adorable," I said.

She stuck her nose in the air as though to say, "What do you mean 'were'?"

I grabbed a handful of the pictures that were still in the box. She hadn't sorted these yet. I was in some of them. I ached when I looked at a picture of my parents, Aunt Erma, and I huddled around a cake on my sixth birthday. I had wanted a cake shaped like a pony. Aunt Erma and my mother baked me a pony cake, and my father frosted it. It was beautiful, and to this day, I remember it as being the most delicious cake I've ever eaten.

I flipped to the next picture. It was a snapshot of Aunt Erma with her arms around some man. I studied it closer. The man's mouth was smiling, but his eyes were sharp. I hadn't ever seen him before, but the two of them sure looked cozy.

"Who is this?" I asked Mitzy. Mitzy went over to the corner and laid down in her bed with her back to me.

In the picture, Aunt Erma was wearing a green teardrop necklace. I had seen that necklace somewhere before.

I glanced at the clock. I had to go meet Henry. I put on three pairs of fleece lined leggings, a tank top and two long sleeve shirts, a heavy grey sweater tunic, my red coat with a green scarf, and a red hat. I put on a pair of regular socks and then a pair of wool socks over those and shoved my feet into my boots. I topped off the look with both gloves and my green mittens just to be safe.

The ice show was at the outdoor ice rink where Henry and I had our first pre-date just a few weeks ago. Henry and I had played hockey. I won the game by a landslide, and he had to buy drinks at Sal's afterward. I had to admit I was a little excited to go back to the scene where sparks had first flown between us.

The ice rink was even more beautiful than I remembered it. There were still Christmas lights hanging on the trees that surrounded the clearing. They had hung even more twinkling lights on poles around the ice rink and had brought in spotlights and bleachers. It was really a nice set up. It, of course, would have been even nicer if it was about fifty degrees warmer outside.

People were already gathering and buying their tickets and hot chocolate from Wally the hot chocolate guy. I hoped that the night would be all about watching ice skating and not about saving everyone from evil magic. Violet was still trying to minimize the problem so people in town wouldn't panic. I wasn't sure if that was the right thing to do or not, but I was too new in town to disagree with her.

"Hey, you," I heard Henry's voice behind me. I gave him a hug.

"If these kids aren't good, we can go out there and show them how it's done," I joked.

A woman passing by shot me an evil glare. Clearly her child was one of the skaters. "Just kidding," I called after her. "Geez these skating parents are intense," I said to Henry.

"Oh, you have no idea," he said shaking his head. He lowered his voice and leaned in. "I heard that several parents were kicked out of ice show rehearsals for getting too involved."

I would have to try to keep my hilarious comments to myself. I was afraid of incurring the wrath of a skating parent almost as much as I was afraid of the IMPs. We bought our tickets and a couple of paper cups of hot chocolate.

"Can I buy a couple more of these to pour over my body?" I asked Henry holding up my steaming cup. He raised his eyebrows. "Wait, that came out wrong," I said laughing. I got another glare from a man sitting in front of us.

"There are children around," he said sharply.

"Sorry," I said. "I just meant I was cold. Maybe I should buy a couple cups for you to pour on your soul." I smiled and took a sip of my hot chocolate.

"You are going to keep everyone on their toes, aren't you?" Henry asked. I shrugged innocently.

The lights in the crowd dimmed and spotlights lit the ice. A Christmas medley played and the whole cast came out wearing red outfits trimmed in white fur. I became so absorbed in their performance, I almost forgot we were watching out for the IMPs. I scanned the crowd looking for someone or something amiss. When I glanced over at Henry, I could tell he was watching everything all at once without looking like he was watching everything. He was almost too good at this. I wondered how many stakeouts he'd been on in his life. Was this a regular thing in this magical town?

I wanted to ask him, but the last thing I needed was Mr. Frigid in front of us glaring at me again, so I just examined the crowd some more. The advanced skaters were on the ice now, doing jumps and spins I had only ever dreamed about doing. I had three years of ice skating lessons under my belt, and that was enough to fuel my Olympic aspirations. My commitment to the sport faltered when I realized that falling hurt, and it would only get worse the higher I jumped.

I saw movement out of the corner of my eye and turned my head. It was him. The man from Aunt Erma's picture. At least I think it was. The spotlight swept across his face, and I was sure. He was older, but he had the same sharp eyes. I leapt out of my seat.

"What are you…" Henry began to ask, but I was hurrying down the bleachers.

"Hey," a couple people called as I bumped them on my way down. I hated bleachers. They were really hard to escape from in a timely manner. And Henry and I had sat near the back so that we would have a good view of the whole crowd.

I made eye contact with the man for only a second, and he hurried away. I rushed after him. I was trying to run discreetly, which wasn't easy. I was getting closer. I was almost close enough to tap him on the shoulder of his tan coat.

"Excuse me," I tried, but he didn't turn around. Suddenly my feet weren't under me anymore. I was airborne for a second. It would have been fun if I hadn't known what was coming next. I landed hard. I heard a crack.

"Are you OK?" A group of people surrounded me.

"Yup," I lied, but I didn't get up. Pain was shooting through my foot.

Henry crouched down next to me within seconds. "Are you OK?"

"I fell on the triple axel," I said with a slight groan. I contemplated standing up. "I think we should go." The crowd was still watching me. I grabbed Henry's hand, and a couple other people were quick to help me up. I drew my breath in sharply when I put weight on my right foot. Yup, that hurt. People were staring, and I didn't want to make any more of a scene than I already had.

"Please get me out of here," I whispered, holding tightly onto Henry's arm. He murmured some words, and I felt my body become lighter. It didn't hurt as much, and I was able to walk out of there.

"Did you see something?" he asked in a low voice.

"Not exactly," I said.

Once we were out of the crowd, he picked me up and carried me. "This would be really romantic if I didn't feel like a total klutz," I said. I explained about the man from the picture. "I don't know who he is, but I feel like there's something going on with Aunt Erma, and I need to figure it out. This guy is a missing piece of the puzzle."

I showed him the picture on my phone, but he didn't know who the man was.

"Hopefully it will all become clear soon. Erma is a powerful woman. She probably knows lots of people, and to be honest, she's just kind of a strange person. She's entitled to a little kookiness with all that she goes through," he said. "And you're entitled to a little kookiness too."

Henry got me back to the pie shop and put me down in a chair out front. My mother was gone, but Aunt Erma was there. Holly appeared at the door seconds after we arrived.

"What did you do to her?" she demanded to Henry pointing at me.

Henry held his hands up. "This was all her doing. She fell doing her triple axel."

"Have you gone to the doctor?" she asked.

"No that's not necessary," I said. The swelling was pushing on my boot, and the pain wasn't going away. "I probably just need to ice it."

Aunt Erma bent down at my feet. She very gently touched my foot. I felt guilty for thinking that she could be up to something.

"I think it's broken. We should probably take her to see Dr. Gabel," she said.

"Can't you just magic it better?" I asked.

"No, healing magic can be tricky, especially with bones. If you do it wrong, it can be really hard to fix," Henry said. "Sorry gimpy."

The doctor confirmed my fear that I'd broken my foot. He prescribed ice, rest, and a very stylish gray walking cast.

Chapter 15

Dear Elodie,

I recently got into a fight with my best friend. He borrowed a couple of books months ago. Since then, I've asked if I could have the books back several times, but he keeps putting off returning them. I finally snapped. It was one of those perfect storm arguments that starts about nothing and then explodes with both sides saying hurtful things they shouldn't.

I have since apologized for the things I said. I told him I would still really like the books back. He said he forgave me, but he hasn't returned the books, and he hasn't apologized for the terrible things he said.

I find myself turning down his invitations to hang out or dodging his phone calls. How can we fix this bump in our friendship? And how do I get my books back?

Sincerely,
Forgive or Fume?

Dear Forgive or Fume?

My question to you is why do you want to fix this friendship? From what you've said, this guy is dismissive about your feelings and your possessions. Talk to him about your argument, and address the things he said that hurt you. Sometimes people are blind to their own mistakes, and he may honestly not recognize that he owes you an apology too. If he still *ignores your concerns, it might be time to cut ties and search for healthier relationships.*

As for the books, my mother always told me you should never lend out something you want back. My guess is that he lost the books, but a best friend should own up to that and offer to replace them.

Ask and I'll Answer,
Elodie

Violet assigned me security camera duty. I was supposed to sit, watch the screen, and call her if I saw Dennis, Brenda, or Stan, or anything that looked suspicious. "How did this happen?" she asked when she came over to drop off the computer I needed to watch security cameras.

"I slipped," I shrugged, but I couldn't look her in the eye. She had laser eyes that I was pretty sure would be able to see the truth if I looked into them.

I set up at a table in the front of the pie shop with my foot wrapped in an ice pack and propped up on a chair. My back was against the wall so none of the customers who came in would be able to see the screen. Not that it really mattered if they could anyway. It was pretty boring stuff.

I could see kids having a snowball fight outside of a school. A bicyclist was locking up her bike. Several people were walking down streets with shopping bags. A paper cup was blowing in the wind. A few people had taken their dogs out to relieve themselves. I saw one man walking down the street with his untied shoelace flopping on the ground. It was an accident waiting to happen, but I was pretty sure Violet didn't want me to call and tell her about it. I watched the cycling security footage intently at first. No IMP activity would go unnoticed on my watch.

133

My mother was at the pie shop again today. It was good she was in town since I was much less helpful now. Despite my weakened state, she still managed to work in three passive aggressive comments and two outright insults about my outfit. She did, however, serve me coffee along with her insults, so glass half full.

After about twenty minutes, I was wishing that I could watch some soap operas or something instead of just security camera footage. I stared blankly at the screen. Focus, Susie, I tried to tell myself, and I shifted in my seat. I might need a lot of coffee to get through this.

I got up a couple times to serve customers, but I was more of a hindrance than a help. I dropped forks and served upside down slices of pie because balancing on one foot and scooping pie was difficult. The doctor told me I could put weight on my broken foot, but it hurt every time I tried. I wanted to break her foot and see if she could put weight on it.

Henry stopped by a little after noon. "I come bearing sustenance," he said, holding out a large brown paper bag. He'd brought my favorite grilled veggie sandwiches from the diner. "There's enough in there for your mom and Erma too," he said. "Unless you're really hungry, and then they never have to know."

"Hey, I heard that," Aunt Erma yelled from the kitchen.

"Please tell me you have some time to hang out." I pulled him down into the chair next to me.

"I think I can spare a few minutes," he said. He updated me on everything that was happening at the nursing home while I ate my sandwich. There was a little holiday romance happening between Frank and Claire. Henry overheard Frank asking around trying to get Claire's name in the Secret Santa exchange.

My phone rang, and I answered without checking the caller ID.

"Susie, it's Buster Hopkins from Top-Notch Construction. I was just calling to see if you've considered my job offer. We'd really like you to start after the holidays."

"I really appreciate the offer," I said. I glanced at Henry. He was watching me intently. "I think I'm going to have to say…"

Buster interrupted before I could finish. "You hold onto that thought. I want you to think about it for a few more days. I think I can even get you a little more paid vacation time than we talked about last time. Talk to you later." He hung up.

"You got a job offer?" he asked.

"Yeah, from a company in the city. I don't plan on taking it though," I said.

"Why didn't you tell me?"

"I didn't think it was a big deal," I shrugged.

"Or maybe you were thinking about taking it?" It was part statement, part question.

I didn't respond fast enough, and he stood up. "I have to get back to work," he said.

Just then, Josh walked in. He gave Henry a little wave. Henry narrowed his eyes at him and left.

My mother was peaking around the kitchen doorway. Now she knew about the job offer. Great.

Josh came over and sat down across from me.

"I heard you were hobbling around, so I brought ice cream." He put a paper cup and a spoon down in front of me.

"Thank you," I said, taking a bite. I let the creamy chocolate scoop melt on my tongue. I told him the edited version about my fall. I left out the fact that I was chasing a man I'd recognized from one of Aunt Erma's photos.

My mother came out to talk to Josh, and within the first ten seconds of the conversation, she managed to work in the fact that I'd gotten a job offer from Top-Notch Construction.

Josh's eyes lit up. I was going to tell them both that I wasn't planning on taking the job, but the two of them went off on a conversation about my future that didn't seem to require any input from me. I stopped paying much attention and started watching the camera feed on the computer again.

Then I saw him. I recognized his coat and his fast, smooth walk. I tried to zoom in on the picture, but it was grainy. I was pretty sure it was him. The guy from the photo. The tag on the corner of the security camera said he was in the next town over. He paused on the sidewalk, looked both ways, and then crossed the street and went through the door of a coffee shop.

My mother got up to serve some customers. I put my walking cast on.

"Where are you going? I'll come with you," Josh offered.

I closed the computer and stood up. "No need," I said. "We'll catch up later." I mouthed to my mom that I would be back soon, and I limped out the door without looking back. Josh followed me out.

"How are you going to drive?" he asked. He pointed at my foot.

He had a point. I hadn't thought about that. I really could use a ride. I would just have to come up with a plan to get him out of the coffee shop once we got there.

"Sure, if you wouldn't mind that would be great. Thanks," I said.

"So where are we going and why can't we tell your family?" he asked. I had almost forgotten how well he knew me.

"I have this meeting at a coffee shop," I said. My mind was racing. "I'm going for an interview. I don't want Aunt Erma to know because, you know, awkward."

He nodded. "Sure. Is the family time too much?"

"Yes," I said, but I could feel that it was forced. I was loving the family time. I still sometimes questioned my baking skills, but not my love for the job. I felt disloyal to Aunt Erma for even saying this.

The drive was nice. We caught up on everything that was happening back home. I was beginning to relax and not think about how he had proclaimed his love or how I was on my way to meet with a man I didn't know.

"Can we get back to our earlier conversation?" he asked the moment there was a lull. We were at a stoplight, and he turned to look at me. His eyes gazed intently.

How did I let a lull happen? I should have kept talking. I should have asked him questions about everyone we ever met just to keep this conversation from happening.

"I really should focus on my interview," I said. "We're almost there."

He sighed and turned his eyes back to the road.

Chapter 16

I sat in the truck for a minute after we pulled into a parking spot. We could just turn around and go back to the pie shop. Maybe I wasn't supposed to find out Aunt Erma's secret. Maybe there wasn't even a secret to find out. There could be a perfectly logical explanation for the strange voicemail, Aunt Erma's odd behavior, and this man from the photo who was suddenly lurking around. All this IMP stuff had me on high alert, and maybe I was creating drama where there wasn't any.

Josh was watching me. "Remember to mention all the marketing you did at Hal's during that holiday promotion," he said.

"Right, the 'Give the gift of straight shelves' campaign," I said with a laugh. "Everyone loves shelves, but most people hate to hang them. Don't hesitate to call Hal's Handyman Services." I gave him an overly enthusiastic thumbs up after running through part of the commercial I'd written for Hal. I had told Josh I was interviewing for a marketing job. It was the first thing that came to mind.

"You're going to be great in there," he said.

"Thanks." I opened the car door. Josh got out too. I froze. "I can't bring a buddy to an interview," I said.

"I'll sit at a different table. You won't even know I'm here. I just want to make sure you don't slip on your way in," he said. I finally agreed because the more I fought it, the more suspicious he was getting.

"Just sit far away so you don't make me nervous," I said.

I held my breath as Josh held the door. I scanned the faces in the shop. It was one of those large warehouse spaces with cement floors and exposed beams in the ceiling. There were two large wooden tables and several smaller ones where people were working on their laptops.

He was still there. Sitting at a small table in the back corner staring at his phone was the man from the picture.

"Do you want a cup of coffee?" Josh asked.

I shook my head. The last thing I needed was coffee. I was already feeling anxious and jittery. He nodded and went to the counter order himself a cup.

I approached the table. His white hair was slicked back, and I could see streaks of the dark brown hair that he had in the picture. His bushy gray eyebrows were pinched together as he typed furiously on his phone. He wore the same tan coat he had on at the ice show. He hadn't taken it off even though it was plenty warm in here. I stood over him until he looked up. He looked annoyed for a minute before recognition swept over his face.

"You look like her, you know," he said, then studied me as though debating his next move. I had him pinned in the corner. His only way out would be to push me down. "Sit." He nodded to the chair across from him.

I sat. I really wished I had prepared better for this meeting. I shouldn't have been chatting so much in the car. I pulled out my phone where I had the picture of the photograph of Aunt Erma and this man.

"Is this you?" I asked. It was obvious it was. Unless he was going to pull the "I have an evil twin" thing.

He nodded.

"How do you know my aunt?"

"Don't you know who I am?" he asked. He said it in a way that made me really wish I did know who he was. I shook my head. I took a moment to glance over and make sure Josh wasn't sitting anywhere near us. He was at a table across the room playing on his phone and drinking a large cup of coffee.

Great. Josh could never handle his caffeine. I would be barraged with show tunes the whole drive back. Or worse, his impersonations of actors, musicians, and talk show hosts. He would go on and on and there was no stopping him when he had this much coffee in his system.

"Who are you? Do you know Dennis and Brenda? Or Stan?" I asked.

He took a deep breath. He was interrupted by a pitch pipe. A group by the front door began singing "Deck the Halls." They were wearing Santa hats and red capes. I'd forgotten we were still in a small town and things like this happened. They were loud carolers, and we had to pause our discussion for a minute. Finally, they finished. I joined in the applause, but the man sitting across from me did not. He just stared into his coffee cup until it was all over.

"I'm Ivan Price," he said once the noise died down. He seemed to be looking for a reaction.

"How do you know my aunt?"

"Erma and I were . . ." he paused for a second. "Close for a while. Probably almost twenty years ago. We were doing some amazing things back then. Making real changes. I've been trying to get a hold of her, but she's been dodging me."

"Maybe you should leave her alone," I said.

"It's not like everything that's been happening to Erma is completely unwarranted," Ivan said.

"What do you mean?" I was instantly defensive.

He laughed, which made me even more angry. "You don't know that much about Erma, do you?"

My face felt hot, and I wondered if I could spill his coffee on him without making a big scene.

"She hasn't always been the good fairy of Hocus Hills, you know," he said. "Her magic hasn't always been so innocent. Why do you think everyone is after her?"

I always thought it was because she was so powerful.

"We want her back on our side. We could make major strides improving the lives of magical people if she came back to our side and quit hiding at her pie shop."

My head was spinning. Was he just trying to mess with me? Aunt Erma had never been involved with the IMPs. She definitely would have told me in one of our drunken late-night chat sessions. Definitely, I told myself.

He took a smug sip of his coffee.

"Why should I believe you?"

"Let me see that picture again," he said. I pulled it up on my phone and showed it to him. "See that necklace she's wearing?" I looked at the green teardrop necklace. "All the IMPs wear them. It was actually Erma's idea. They connect us." He reached under his white button up shirt and pulled out an identical necklace to the one in the picture. It had a sinister glow, and I leaned back in my chair. Then it hit me. I knew where else I'd seen that necklace. Nellie had been wearing the same one.

"So you're one of them." I couldn't keep the disgust out of my tone.

"One of them?" He laughed. "I'm not just one of them. I started the movement. Well, with Erma's help. I'm Ivan Michael Price, founder of the Improvement of Magical People."

I realized my mouth was hanging open, so I closed it.

"Things kind of died off for a while. People lost interest. But now that we're picking up steam again, we either need Erma back or at the very least figure out where she gets her power. No one else can do what she does. There has to be a secret."

For the first time, I felt like I might actually be in danger. I didn't want Ivan to try and get Aunt Erma's secret out of me. What if he put a truth spell on me?

I glanced across the room to check on Josh again. He wasn't at his table. He was looking through a stack of

141

newspapers at a table not too far away from where I was sitting. How long had he been there? Could he hear what we were talking about? We had to get out of here.

I stood up quickly. "Nice to meet you, Mr. Price," I said loudly. Ivan made a move to stand up. "No," I said sharply. He fell back in his chair as though I'd knocked him over. His eyes were wide for a second, then he smiled slightly.

"I see you take after your aunt," he said.

I didn't give him the chance to say anything else. I hurried out the door. I was halfway back to the car before Josh caught up to me.

"Hey," he gently grabbed my arm as he caught up to me. "Are you OK?"

"Of course," I said, flashing him a smile, but I could feel the smile waver a little.

He began humming the song, "Maybe," from *Annie* and I braced myself for the full on singing outburst. It didn't come though. "I was definitely not trying to listen in," Josh said when we got into the truck. "But I may have overheard a thing or two, and it sounded like you guys were having some strange conversation. What is that? Some new kind of interviewing technique?"

"He was a strange guy," I said. "Apparently everyone in the company wears matching necklaces, and he kept going on and on about how they try to create magic wherever they go. A little too hippy dippy for me."

He started the truck. "So, what's the plan then?" he asked, casually.

"I think I'm going to stay at the pie shop for a while." I looked out the window, so I didn't have to look at his face. I was silent for a minute. "I got an apartment in Hocus Hills."

He let out a long slow breath. "Is this your way of saying you don't love me?" he asked.

142

"I don't love you like you want me to. I love you like a best friend," I said. I saw his fingers tighten around the steering wheel. I wished that we weren't having this conversation in a car like this. I wanted to give him a hug. Yet part of me was relieved not to have to face him. I watched the car in front of us too.

"We're so good together," he said.

"But romance has always been hard for us. We've never been on the same page at the same time. It shouldn't be that hard. Not from the beginning," I said. We pulled into a parking spot near the pie shop. Josh turned off the truck and looked down at the keys in his hand. "We've always been better suited as friends. I've missed you, but I've been selfish leading you on because I like your company."

"You've always been selfish," he said. He got out of the truck, shut the door hard, and walked away.

I sat there frozen for a minute. My heart was pounding. I tried not to cry. I didn't want to start, but once the first tear was out, there was no stopping the rest from following. I cried for Josh. I cried for Aunt Erma and the years we weren't together and the things she may have done. I cried for another Christmas without my dad.

There was a tap at the window. Darn these small towns. I wiped my face on the sleeve of my coat and looked over to see Henry's concerned face peering in at me. I tried to pull myself together as I opened the door, but instead, a fresh wave of tears came. He didn't ask me what was wrong, he just wrapped me in his arms and let me cry.

Chapter 17

My meltdown didn't last too long. I had questions to ask Aunt Erma. I pulled away from Henry and started laughing.

"What?" he looked alarmed like I might have actually fallen off my rocker this time. He was twisted awkwardly so he could hug me.

"How are you holding that position?" I asked in a tearful giggle.

"I sneak into yoga sometimes," he said. He straightened up with a slight groan. "Maybe I should sneak into some more classes." He pulled a handkerchief out of his pocket, because apparently, he was a gentlemen from the eighteen hundreds. I wiped my face and blew my nose.

"Here," I said with a wicked smile as I handed him the dirty handkerchief back.

"Thanks." To my surprise he took it and put it back in his pocket. I was touched and repulsed at the same time. I told Henry about my conversation with Josh. He somehow managed to look angry, sympathetic, and relieved all at the same time.

"You are the least selfish person I know. He shouldn't have said that to you. But if he feels even a fraction of what I feel for you, I can imagine how awful he must have felt when you told him you don't feel the same way," Henry said. "But that doesn't excuse his behavior," he added quickly.

"I just hope Josh and I can be friends again someday," I said.

"I hope you can too." Henry gave me another squeeze, and we went inside.

Violet was there talking to my mother.

"Where have you been?" my mother asked. When she noticed I'd been crying she asked, "What's wrong?" Then she turned sharply to Henry. "What did you do to her?"

"It's nothing, Mom. My foot just hurts a little," I said. "I was out running some errands. I was a little too ambitious about how far I could walk in this thing." I pointed to the walking cast on my foot. "Henry helped me back." This would all probably come out as a lie at some point. I'm sure someone in town saw me in the truck with Josh, and probably at least one person saw me crying on Henry's shoulder from their window. I would deal with that later.

"Is everything OK?" Henry asked Violet.

"Have either of you seen Erma in the last couple hours?"

We both shook our heads. "Why?" I asked.

"There's been some chatter that the IMPs are going to try something big. I came to warn Erma, but when I got here, your mother said she'd stepped out for a minute," Violet said.

"She's not answering her cell phone, and we're afraid they got to her," my mother said.

I had a sinking feeling in my stomach. Or maybe she went back to their side. I wasn't sure if I should tell Violet and my mother what I learned from Ivan. I decided against it. She was still my aunt after all, and if she didn't go to join the IMPs, I would be tarnishing her reputation for no reason.

Violet decided she needed to call in the Morning Pie Crew.

"I need their help searching for Erma, but we need to keep a low profile," she said. "We don't want the rest of the town to realize how dire the situation is. A bunch of magical people panicking would just make this all even more dangerous."

I had an idea where Aunt Erma might be, but I had to get out of the pie shop without raising suspicions.

Flora, Lena, and Mr. Barnes got to the pie shop quickly. Violet filled them in while my mother called Aunt Erma's cell phone repeatedly. I told her that Aunt Erma often forgets to turn on her cell phone or leaves it in the car, but my mother kept trying anyway. Not that I blamed her. It was strange for Aunt Erma to be gone so long on one of our busy days before the holiday. It was even stranger that no one had seen her during that time.

Henry helped me serve any customers that came in. Some people looked over at the group huddled around the table with raised eyebrows. "They're planning a Christmas surprise," I would say with a bright smile, and everyone seemed to accept that explanation.

The Morning Pie Crew left to go on their mission to find Aunt Erma. Violet gave my mother and I strict instructions to stay at the pie shop in case Aunt Erma came back. Plus, we had to make sure everything appeared as normal as possible to the townspeople.

"Of course, we'll stay here," I assured Violet. But in my head, I was thinking, "Fat chance." She nodded, satisfied and left.

As though on cue, the dogs started barking upstairs. "I'd better take them on a walk," I told my mother.

"I'll help," Henry offered and followed me upstairs.

Mitzy danced around our feet, and Duncan was on the sofa under my blanket with his head on my pillow.

"Hey, get off of there," I scolded. "You have a dog bed for a reason." He reluctantly dragged himself off the sofa.

"Do you trust me?" I asked Henry.

"Of course," he said.

"I need to go out for a little bit. I can't tell you where I'm going. Can you cover for me?"

"Are you going to do something dangerous?" he asked.

146

I hesitated. "Hopefully not too dangerous." There was the part of me that desperately wanted Henry to come along, but I still felt like I had to keep the tree a secret. What if Aunt Erma really was just out doing some Christmas shopping or something? What if the IMPs had no idea there even was a magic tree? I couldn't burden him with this secret and betray Aunt Erma's trust until I knew more.

"Can you at least take Duncan with you? I'd feel better if you had a guard dog along," he said.

I looked over at Duncan. He let out a gigantic yawn and blinked sleepily at us. "Him? You'd feel better if I had him along?" I asked.

Henry smiled, "Yes."

"Fine, I'll bring him along."

"Can you drive with that thing?" He nodded to my walking cast.

"I'll find a way," I said confidently. I hoped he couldn't hear my heart pounding in my chest.

"OK. Call me if you need anything," he said. He held my gaze for a minute and then we kissed.

I said goodbye and left with Duncan sluggishly following me. He seemed happy do discover we were going on a car ride not a walk.

I took the walking cast off when we got to the car. It hurt to press the pedals, but it wasn't unbearable. I cranked up the Christmas music to distract myself from the pain. Duncan watched out the window for a few minutes, but soon he was sprawled across the back seat snoring loudly. "You're supposed to provide protection," I reminded him, but he didn't wake up.

As we drove, I wondered if Aunt Erma would have really brought the IMPs to the magic tree. I hoped I was about to prove all of my suspicions wrong. I turned down the dirt road, and I saw her car parked off to the side. This wasn't where the tree

147

was. I parked a little ways away, though it was hard to hide on this deserted road. Duncan perked up when the car stopped.

"You should wait in the car," I said. He leapt over the front seat and followed me out the door before I could stop him.

There were multiple sets of footprints in the snow starting at Aunt Erma's car. We followed them. Duncan grabbed the corner of my coat with his teeth. I was about to scold him when I heard voices.

"I think I'm all turned around." It was Aunt Erma.

"Stan followed your niece out to these woods. We know your magic comes from something in here," a woman's voice said. It sounded like Brenda.

"Yes, and I want to share it with you. I think I turned at the wrong rock," Aunt Erma said. "Maybe we should go back this way."

"We've already been that way," a man's voice said.

"We're going to find it with or without you," Brenda said. "More IMPs are on their way, and we'll search the entire woods."

I turned and hurried back to the car with Duncan close at my heels.

Aunt Erma was doing her best to distract them. "We can't let them find the tree," I said when we got back to the car. Duncan wagged his tail in agreement. Aunt Erma derived a lot of power just from harvesting small portions of the tree. The IMPs wouldn't exercise the same restraint once they felt that much magic. The destruction they could do to our magical community was almost unimaginable.

I drove further down the road until I was at the spot closest to the tree. Duncan and I got out of the car. I went around to the trunk and grabbed my tool bag. I unzipped it. The axe was smaller than I would have liked, but it would do the job. I took a deep breath and marched through the woods.

Along the way I called Violet. She sounded distracted when she picked up.

"You're probably going to want to come find me," I said.

"Why? Where are you?" I had her attention now.

"I'm in the woods, and there's about to be a lot of angry IMPs in here," I said. I did my best to give her directions to my location. I got to the tree. "I have to go. I'll tell you more when you get here," I hung up amid her protests.

I put my hand on the trunk of the tree and felt the tingling rush of magic up my arm. The trunk of the tree began to glow. That was new. Duncan sat solemnly behind me.

"I'm sorry," I whispered to the tree.

Then I swung the axe hard against the trunk. I swung again and again. I kept reminding myself this had to be done. I squinted against the flying chunks of wood and worked quickly. The sound of the axe would probably echo through the woods. The IMPs could find me at any moment.

I knew the best way to cut down a tree. When I was in college, I had a huge crush on a guy, Luke, from my English Composition course. Luke competed in lumberjack competitions. I was his number one fan for a couple months until I realized I would never be anything more than his number one fan. But while I was there I picked up a lot of tips on the fastest way to chop down a tree. The universe works in mysterious ways.

My arms were burning, and sweat was dripping down my back. I threw my coat off and kept chopping. I could feel blisters forming under my gloves. Duncan was walking in circles now. He was on high alert, keeping his eyes open for uninvited guests.

When I was on what felt like my thousandth swing, I vowed that I would start keeping a chainsaw in the trunk of my car. The glow of the tree was beginning to fade. Duncan stretched and yawned as though he wished I would hurry so he could get back to his nap, but he never stopped watching the surrounding trees.

Duncan began to growl. I was almost all the way through the trunk.

"Stop," a voice cried. I glanced over. It was Ivan. His hair wasn't slicked back anymore. It stuck out to the sides and hung in his face. He was out of breath. "Get away from the tree."

I froze for a second. His eyes had a dangerous glint. Brenda, Dennis, Stan, and Aunt Erma all appeared between the trees. Duncan's growling got more vicious.

I threw myself at the tree.

"Noooo!" Ivan cried.

I heard Brenda yelling something, and everything went black.

When I came to, I was looking up into Henry's worried eyes.

"Is this a dream?" I asked, reaching towards his face. "Because if it is, it's a good one."

He cracked a small smile, but his brow was still furrowed. "How do you feel?" he asked.

"Like someone knocked me out with a spell," I groaned. "But otherwise fantastic."

I felt something on top of my stomach. It was furry. I looked down, and Duncan was resting his head on me. He was whining softly.

"It's OK, buddy," I said. I moved my arm to pet him, and I felt leaves brush against the back of my hand. The tree was on the ground. I did it! I knocked it over before I passed out. The IMPs wouldn't ever be able to get to the magic now. The trunk wasn't glowing anymore. I reached out to touch the nearest branch. It felt cold against my fingers. Tears prickled in my eyes.

There was some yelling, and I sat up quickly to see what the commotion was all about. I felt woozy.

"Careful." Henry grabbed my shoulders.

Violet, the Morning Pie Crew, and several Magic Enforcement Officers were there detaining the IMPs. Brenda was yelling at Dennis and Stan, and Ivan was yelling at Brenda. From what I could gather, Brenda blamed Dennis and Stan for not finding the tree sooner. Ivan blamed Brenda for scaring away half of their IMP recruits with her off-putting personality.

They were detained in magic handcuffs. They looked like regular handcuffs, but Henry explained that they couldn't do magic while they were wearing them. Stan almost looked relieved to be caught. Maybe magic jail would be a better place for him, as long as he didn't end up in a cell next to his mother.

They were lining up more people in handcuffs. People I didn't recognize.

"Those are other IMPs. They were in the woods looking for this, apparently," Henry said, pointing to the tree. "What exactly is this?"

I told him about the tree. It didn't seem like I had to keep the secret anymore. "I'm sorry I didn't tell you earlier," I said.

"I understand why you didn't," he said, pulling a twig out of my hair.

I was still sitting on the ground, and Henry was crouched next to me when Aunt Erma walked towards us. My stomach did a flip.

"I'm sorry about your tree," I said.

She crouched down in front of me. "You did exactly what you had to do. You saved us all. If the IMPs had gotten a hold of the tree, it would have been catastrophic. I'm very proud of you," she said firmly.

I blinked back tears and nodded.

"Now here, eat this," Aunt Erma handed me a taffy. "It should make you feel better."

I put it in my mouth and the queasy feeling faded. "What exactly are in these?" I asked as I chewed.

She smiled at me. "I still have one or two secrets up my sleeve."

Henry offered to drive me home, and Aunt Erma said she would stay and help Violet.

Once we were in the car, Duncan leaned over the front seat and rested his head on my shoulder. I felt more love for him than I ever thought would be possible to feel for a dog.

"Do you think Aunt Erma is capable of doing bad magic?" I asked.

Henry paused for a minute. "I think everyone is capable of doing bad magic," he said.

Exhaustion set in, and the minute we got back to the apartment I stumbled to the sofa and collapsed. Duncan carefully climbed in next to me. I didn't bother to shoo him out. He opted to be the big spoon. I mumbled goodnight to Henry and was out.

Chapter 18

I straightened the wreath on the door. I felt the familiar thrill of Christmas run through me. Everyone was coming to my new apartment to celebrate. Duncan and I had moved in a couple days ago. Aunt Erma, my mother, Flora, Lena, Mr. Barnes, Holly, and Henry had all helped me move, so it only took about five minutes. I didn't have much stuff yet.

I'd gone back to my apartment in the city and sold a lot of my things after it became apparent that I would be in Hocus Hills for a while. So I was mostly starting from scratch here, and I liked that.

Flora had an old bed I could use, and Lena and I built a table out of some of the wood from the magic tree. Aunt Erma gave me lots of twinkle lights to hang around the apartment. I'd found an overstuffed blue chair at the consignment shop. When I sat in the chair, I felt like I was sitting in a cloud. That was all the furniture in my apartment so far. So, Christmas was going to be a bring your own chair event.

On moving day my mother brought me a potted plant and a healthy dose of motherly guilt. "Are you sure this apartment is a good idea?" she asked. "It's just so…permanent."

My mother had gotten the gist of what happened out in the woods even though I'd tried to sugar coat the story for her. She doubled down on her efforts to get me back to the city.

"It's a month to month lease, Mom. And yes, I'm sure," I said, giving her a hug.

Aunt Erma came back the first night in my new apartment with a bottle of champagne. We hadn't had much chance to talk since the day in the woods. I had some questions for her about the things Ivan had said.

"Quite a week we've had." She popped the cork while I stared at the few dishes in my cupboards.

"More exciting than most I've had," I said. I opted for the chipped mugs I'd swiped from the pie shop.

We clinked our mugs and sat down. I sat cross legged on the bed and Aunt Erma sat in the blue chair.

"Ivan said he told you some things about my past. Some things I was hoping you'd never find out," she started. I nodded and took a sip of champagne as I waited for her to continue. "Your father was one of my best friends. After he died, your mother forbid me from ever seeing you or her again because she blamed me for not trying to save him with magic."

I nodded again. I'd heard this part before, but I had a feeling she had to ease into the story for her sake as much as mine.

"I was lost. Everything I'd held onto before, the things that stabilized me, the people who made my life make sense, were gone."

"Did you ever try to talk to Mom again? After Dad died?" I asked.

She nodded sadly. "I tried many times over the years to talk to her, but she always refused to let me back in." She picked a couple dog hairs off the blue chair. "While I don't agree with her decision to cut me out, I know she was in so much pain after your father died. She was lost too." She took a breath. "I was at my lowest point when I met Ivan. He had just lost his sister. We were both looking for a new beginning, and we understood each other in a way I didn't know if I would ever find again."

I stood and refilled both of our mugs with champagne.

"I can't pinpoint exactly when things got out of control. We were both a little bitter and felt like we deserved better. More people joined us. We formed a sort of family I suppose. The magic we were doing seemed harmless at first. We took some

154

things we wanted. Small stuff. We would control non-magic people for just for a few minutes here and there to get our way. To get free drinks or a table at a restaurant. I don't know when it became bigger. It was gradual. Mr. Barnes saved me from that life. The others don't even know about it," she said. "He saw me put a spell on a man, so I could steal his car." She glanced at me. "I know, not my proudest moment. Anyway, he reminded me that I could do good things with my magic. He has a way of making the world sound beautiful and hopeful. He brought me to Hocus Hills. I opened the pie shop and never looked back."

"Didn't Ivan ever come looking for you before now?" I asked.

She shook her head. "I assumed he moved on with his life too. I heard the IMPs still existed, but I hadn't heard from him until his voice was on my answering machine."

"Did you consider going back to the IMPs?" I couldn't look at her when I asked the question, but I needed the answer.

"No," she answered firmly. "They were a mistake from my past, they're not a page from my future."

We finished the bottle of champagne that night, and with each clink of our glasses came more love and understanding.

Buster Hopkins had called again to see if I'd reconsidered his offer. I told him I really appreciated it, but I was going to be in Hocus Hills for the foreseeable future.

The only thing left hanging over my head on Christmas morning was Josh. I hated how we ended things, but I pushed that out of my mind, so I could focus on the festivities.

My mother and Aunt Erma came over early to help me make veggie lasagna, mashed potatoes, and four kinds of pie.

Aunt Erma had brought Mitzy along, and Mitzy was staring intently at Duncan's sleeping body as though she could will him to wake up. When subtlety didn't work, she walked over and stepped on his head. He woke up for a moment, sniffed her, and then went back to sleep. Poor Mitzy. She got the short end of the stick when she ended up with Duncan as her best friend.

Once everything was prepared, my mother surveyed our meatless meal and asked if I was sure I was getting enough protein in my diet.

"Yes, Mom," I answered the question for the thousandth time with an audible sigh.

Mr. Barnes arrived with a salad and some candles. "They're made from a mix of essential oils, including lavender, to promote tranquility," he said. I lit them right away.

Lena brought cheese puffs and a bottle of wine. Flora brought a fruit salad and a stack of framed pictures for my walls. She had been making us pose all week, every time we were at the pie shop, and now I knew why. I laughed when I saw the one where Lena had flung a bite of pie at the camera. The camera caught the moment right before blueberries hit the lens. Everyone except Lena was in the background looking shocked. Lena was laughing hysterically.

Holly and her mother Luanne came next. Holly brought chocolates shaped like Santa Claus and Luanne brought something with kale and spinach. She was always critiquing the food I bought at the grocery store and telling me I need to eat more greens.

Violet arrived looking exhausted, but satisfied, and carrying a large basket of garlic bread. She told us they had detained several IMPs, and the rest had gone back underground. We wouldn't be hearing from them for a while. She also lectured Aunt Erma and I again on how dangerous it was to be out in the woods with the IMPs without the Magic Enforcement Team behind us. The first time was right after the day in the woods. Aunt Erma had argued with Violet saying that she had to go in alone.

"If the IMPs had even gotten a whiff of the Magic Enforcement Officers, things could have gotten really ugly really quickly," Aunt Erma told her. But Violet wouldn't have any of it.

I took every lecture with a bowed head and a lot of nodding because I didn't see a point in arguing with Violet. I would never win.

This time she kept her lecture short. She must be in a good mood today.

Henry burst through the door next wearing a Santa hat and carrying a large tray of something covered in powdered sugar in one hand and his guitar in the other. I gave him a kiss, and he held up a bag that was wrapped around his wrist.

"Claire sent over some of her special eggnog. Drink at your own risk," he said.

With ten people and two dogs, my new apartment was at capacity, and I loved it. The room was filled with food and cheerful chattering.

There was a knock at the door. Everyone was here. Who could it be? The room quieted, and they all turned toward the door. Clearly, they were wondering the same thing.

I opened it, and there was Josh looking sheepish and uncomfortable.

"Hi," he said. Then he noticed the packed apartment and he shrank back. Everyone was quiet and staring at him.

"Hi," I said with a sigh. I hadn't told anyone besides Henry and Holly exactly what had happened between Josh and I, but they picked up enough to know that Josh and I weren't speaking anymore. Flora had asked me the other day when Josh would be coming by again because she had a book she wanted to lend him. I'd said, "Don't know. Don't care." The line of questioning stopped there.

"Can I talk to you?" he asked quietly. "Please?"

There was no place to talk privately in the apartment, unless we went into the bathroom. Which would certainly be one way to make an awkward conversation even more awkward. I stepped out to the hallway closing the door behind me.

I walked halfway down the hall before stopping. I knew every ear in the apartment would be pressed against my door the second I closed it. I was tempted to throw it open it just to watch them all scatter.

"What's up?" I asked after we'd stood for a moment in silence.

"First, I wanted to say I'm sorry," he said.

"Oh? For what?" I wasn't going to let him off the hook that easily.

"For coming here and saying I love you without thinking of the repercussions. I should have told you a long time ago. I had no right coming here and messing with your life. Especially since you seem so happy, and Henry seems like such a stand-up guy," he said.

"Yeah, he is," I said. Josh met my eyes for the first time since we'd gone out to the hallway.

"That became even more apparent when he invited me here today," Josh said.

"He invited you?" I was a little surprised. Wow, Henry really was a stand-up guy.

"I'm also very sorry that I called you selfish. I was hurt, and I lashed out, but that's no excuse. I was the one being selfish. I shouldn't have projected that on you. I put you in a terrible spot and I'm sorry," he said.

"Thank you," I said. "And I forgive you."

"My project is almost done, and I'll be leaving to go back home in a couple days," he paused for a breath. "I know we might need a little time apart, but I really hope we can go back to being friends. Maybe I can find my Henry," he smiled a little. "Or Henrietta."

"I'd like our friendship back," I agreed. Though I knew a little time apart wouldn't hurt. "You should come in for dinner though," I said. The time apart could start after Christmas dinner.

He smiled, "I'd like that. Thank you."

Everyone's wide, curious eyes stared at us when we walked through the door.

"Josh is going to join us for dinner," I said with a smile, so everyone would know he was forgiven. My mother looked thrilled.

Flora poured Josh a glass of wine, and he slid right into a conversation with Mr. Barnes and Luanne.

Henry followed me as I went to check on the lasagna in the oven.

"Is everything OK?" he asked in a low voice. The chatter had started up again, so we could talk and not be overheard.

"Yes. Thanks for inviting him here so we could patch things up. All feels right with the world now," I said.

Mr. Barnes began singing Deck the Halls. Henry pulled out his guitar and strummed along. Soon everyone was singing. I tried to blink back my happy tears. I felt so lucky to be a part of this big strange family.

I went to sleep happy that night. I could still feel the warm glow of love and wine. Duncan was snuggled into my back. It would be nice if he didn't snore so loudly. I moved my head a little further from his mouth and drifted off into a deep sleep.

I sat straight up in bed. Duncan reluctantly lifted his head to look at me. I don't know how long I had been asleep. I must have been dreaming, but it was so vivid. I put on my boots and coat. Duncan followed me, his tail wagging.

159

"Are you coming with?" I asked, a little surprised. I thought he would prefer to stay in the cozy bed. His tail wagged harder, so I grabbed his leash.

It was dark and cold outside. I could hear the wind chimes in front of Flora's shop softly jingling in the breeze. I cringed a little as I started my car. I really should get my muffler fixed.

It was still clear in my mind. Usually my dreams, even the ones I tried to remember, faded quickly after I got up. Not this time. It was as though my mind was giving me turn by turn directions. "Turn left in three hundred feet. Turn right at the stoplight. Merge onto the highway." I exited the highway and drove down an asphalt road. The asphalt road turned into a dirt road. The trees got thicker. "Stop," the GPS in my mind said. Duncan and I got out of the car and walked into the woods. The air was quiet except for a few leaves rustling and our feet crunching in the snow.

"We're here," I whispered and dropped to my knees. Duncan crept up slowly behind me. He sniffed the air, but lost interest when he didn't see any food. I gently dug the snow away. There it was. It was small, just a twig sticking out of the ground with a few tiny green leaves growing out of it.

"Hey friend," I whispered. I pulled off my mitten and gently touched one of the leaves. I could feel the tingle of magic.

Made in the USA
San Bernardino, CA
20 December 2017